D1806196

Laden with Flowers

Ben Poppy

This narrative is a work of fiction

It was a cold evening in November, when grandfather's hand struck the hour. W.B Yeats, his fingertips pressing against the table, slowly stood from his chair to announce the first official meeting of the Rhymers Club.
"Gentleman, if you may take your seats."
The room smelt of ale and stale tobacco as a small group of men began to quieten and seat themselves in the chairs provided.
"Gentleman, you have found yourselves here at the Cheshire Cheese tonight for one reason,
   to reclaim our artistry."

A gentle applause gathered in the Fleet Street pub as a landlord and his wife hurriedly locked the doors and pulled shut the curtains.
"An attack has been made upon the beauty of our language, and we must resist!"
 A grand fireplace fuelled their warmth as pipe smoke swirled in their vile air; burning candles graced the mantelpiece as Yeats took a sip of whisky and continued his statement.
"For too long we have kept quiet. For too long we have hidden away, but no longer, we must fight back, with the sharpness of our pens!"
A sea of hands began to slam against the table as Yeats reclaimed his seat. Glasses were clunked together in solidarity, while a young poet stood up with pronounced aggression.

"Sir I must speak out. If we are to fight back then we must do so in the strictest of secrecy. We must not draw unwanted attention; we must not let ourselves be caught!"
Quiet claps, cheers and wide eyes decorated the room as our young poet waited for the silence to be regained once more.
" But don't you see gentleman…, don't you see who we have elected as our leader? A man who holds friendships with the likes of Alistair Crowley? A man obsessed with the magic and mysticism of the beast? Surely my fellow Rhymers, this draws unwanted attention?"

With fierce black eyes the young man took his seat as a crowd of whispers gathered upon the tongue. A portrait of Victoria slept within her frame, while outside lamplighters busied themselves igniting the last lanterns of the night.
"And who may you be sir?" questioned Ernest Rhys as he pulled his chair closer to the table,
"What is your name?"

Furnished with pockets, buckles, waistcoats, chains and smart attire the elders looked at the young man with intensity.

"My name is Sebastian Fanshaw sir."

Sebastian swept back his dark brown hair as the audience conversed against the orange glow of the fire. Ernest sat back, struck a match and lit his pipe.

" Tell me Mr Fanshaw," said Ernest as a trail of smoke relaxed his words, "Tell me, how can a man who is friends with the likes of Oscar Wilde criticize another mans choice of company? A man so flamboyant in his artistry, he commands the eyes of anyone who comes into contact with him. A peacock who stands against the greyness of the sky, a man of free thought. Can you answer me that Mr Fanshaw?"

The spider sat patiently for a kill in the corner of the room as Sebastian turned his gaze towards the ground.

"I can't sir," was the reply sent solemnly.

The sound of passing carriages thundered outside the window as Ernest took another toke from his pipe. "All of us are in danger… we are men of letters….we live in a time when our profession has been outlawed… all of us are being watched."

A cold wind sent a loud roar through the chimney, sending shivers down the spines of everyone present.

" We must create a network of poets….writers…..painters and actors, of Musicians….sculptures...philosophers, dancers and intellects. We must shoulder the burden of fear in the struggle to reclaim beauty. We must unite and bring a city back to life! A city laden with flowers. "

Applause disrupted the room once more as Ernest sat back in his chair. Yeats with his dark brown hair, spectacles and pale skin had been sat in silent contemplation.

"Are you still not happy with me leading the Rhymers Sebastian?" asked Yeats, as he took another sip of whisky.

"I'm happy for you to lead Sir," Sebastian mumbled still looking at the ground.

"You see Mr Fanshaw I have much experience in keeping discreet, belonging to an order whose deeds have been long unlawful. Nothing must be written about the Rhymers, and we must not converse except at our monthly meetings here at the Cheshire Cheese. We are here to plan, organise and hear the deeper thought of word. To keep the flame of verse alive."

"Hear, hear" agreed each member of the club, while their landlord stood quietly behind the bar cleaning glasses.

"The hour is late, and so we must begin our reading," stated Yates. "Joseph

why don't you go first?"
A finely dressed, bearded, middle aged man stood up from the far end of the table and softly cleared his throat.
"Gentleman this is a short but recent work I composed titled *Windily Bay*."

"We rode among the saddened trees
As their branches drained the light
Our morning dead with the shadowed green
And the overture of night

A blessed soul gathers the ground
And returns it to the wood
And in his place we mistake his voice
For the silhouette of youth

The flower cries out from her rooted home
And prays for the morning siege
A hanging crown for the lonesome sun
Who fed her precious seed

The waves crashed against giants
And tides they rehearsed the day
Shells of pain left broken
As we walked upon windily bay…"

A small applause gathered among the men as his words drifted into silence.
Ernest emptied his pipe before sitting up to readdress his fellow writers.
"For those of you who don't know, we are planning an anthology. An anthology with an invisible writer! We will have it printed illegally and use our various networks as distribution. Each of us will contribute poems to the future work. We will keep verse alive…"

"Hear, hear"
Nathanial stood up to begin his reading,

There was a knock on the door. The room became scented in a vile stench of dread. Each man looking at one another with bewilderment and fear as another knock slammed against their hearts.
 "Keep quiet"
The landlord pulled back the bolts from their locks and was greeted by rain, the street and a strange silhouetted figure.

"May I come in?"

The landlord shaking, slowly walked back into the room as the man followed him in. With a lean figure, thick black moustache and handsome features, Inspector Millar wore himself with pride. An elegant but cruel official of her Majesty's police, a sworn enemy of artistry and creativity. His nose was submersed beneath a handkerchief in an effort to avoid the vile smell of urine from the street, an effort owed to his privilege and snobbishness. He closed the door behind him.

"Gentleman what a pleasure it is to see you here tonight," grinned Millar as he walked towards the table,

"What a pleasure."

The rhymers lay trapped with knotted tongues, shuddering to the chill of the night. Our spider had found its prey, and was sitting patient.

"Have you noticed your friend Jacque missing from your assembly here tonight Mr Yeats?" smiled the inspector, as he pulled out a chair and sat himself down, "I presume you have?"

Yeats stared out into the distance, silent and still.

"We picked him up in the early hours of this morning when he was trying to deliver a book, a banned book, I'm sure you're aware, he kept silent for a while but we got him talking."

The fire had begun to shrink and the candlelight was fading. Outside the sound of a dozen police officers was forming.

"He told us of your names, your ambitions, your desires, even of your methods Mr Yeats. I'm aware I will not find any written verse on you gentlemen here tonight, you commend it to memory, to evade capture. He has told us everything…you are all under arrest."

Sebastian shaking with fear shot up and made a run for the door but the inspector lay still and unnerved.

"Officers are standing outside Mr Fanshaw, there is no escape."

Members of the club sat silently and finished their cigarettes while others began to put on their winter coats, ready for the fate that awaited them.

"Please, please don't do this," cried Sebastian. "This is absurd. We do no wrong."

"Ah, but you do Mr Fanshaw, that you do."

The spider caught its prey with vicious precision, slowly wrapping its feast in murderous silk.

The Playwright

The spirit of creativity gripped him, enveloping his heart and turning all his pain into something beautiful, something pure.
"We welcome you to the Painted Theatre," announced Stinky the Clown in his usual attire. "We hope you enjoy the production and shhh… don't tell anyone."
Oil lamps glowed softly against the cardinal red of their intimate surroundings, a chestnut mould submerging all who came to witness William's heart laid bare. Beholding a picture, yet part of it.

"Is it to be or not to be?" muttered the General backstage as the velvet curtain was lifted to unveil a young man at his desk writing. William remembered this period well, and remembered it vividly. The madness of someone who creates good art can always be forgiven. They can exist within their own creation, inside the foundations of their own architecture. He could fall in love from afar, imagining what was and what could've been, a realm of possibilities endless.
He felt a kinship with his audience, together an expression of their sterile and turbulent age. In times when it was important to attend, when it was important to perform.

The theatre forged it's notoriety on the outskirts of a grey vacuous London. A deed owned by an ageing Alfred Douglas, an aristocrat, who the police were reluctant to investigate. In his youth he had been the subject, the inspiration and model to many of London's greatest artists, from Wilde to the underground painters of his day. Blonde, slim and handsome with piercing blue eyes, Douglas stood at the back of the theatre, allowing the performance to unfold.

Charles was playing the part of William with precise precision. Wearing a fine fitting black suit with all the warmth and sadness of his friend becoming exposed through the eyes, his anxiety through the fingertips, pressing nervously against his undernourished legs.
"Will she ever know of my deepest nature? My deepest thoughts? An artist must reveal all to the world, and now must do so…to the woman he loves."
The production consisted of three parts,
Act one: The Beginning
Act two: The Middle
Act three: The Reveal

Each line contained the words of Williams's catharsis, puncturing the audience with a transcending thought, their minds shaping into a captive consciousness. For those short moments he mattered, and above all mattered to the woman he loved.

Isabel.

He remembered the first time he saw her, bright within the shadows of the scarlet theatre. Catching her every laugh, her every tear, he revelled in being puppet master to sensitivity, to the soul. She connected to his work, withdrawing his invisibility, his isolation.

In the bleak existence of reality he mattered to very few, only to Douglas and a loyal troupe of disaffected actors nicknamed The Seeds. He was unable to release his thoughts, his musings, his humour; exiled from all forms of psychical connection.

"This could be the greatest work we've done" whispered Leopold as he came to William's side, wearing a haggard brown suit, large black shoes and patchy clown makeup. "It concerns what really matters."

The narrative of the production was that of his life. His secrets slowly unravelling themselves into the public domain. Panic tightened around his body and mind as William drowned in the realization of what he was doing.

"What will she think?"

Neurotic tremors of self- loathing palpitated through the skin as he became consumed by a soul- crushing inadequacy. A terrifying penance for a self-serving creation.

"William?"

Laughter exhaled into the reign of joyous sound as the performers re-enacted one of their many backstage quarrels. With fights often taking place between Leopold and Stinky in their adolescent and often comical aggression. Each actor recited from their own tongue except for Charles who was happy to become the writer's medium. His friend's manifestation on stage.

"William isn't it?"

The Playwright had been introduced to his angel eyed witness a few weeks before by a charismatic actress Annie.

"It's nice to finally meet you Sir," she smiled as she took a seat backstage. "I've enjoyed everything you've written. Your productions have brought life to a dreaded existence Mr Caswell. I can't thank you enough! I never knew such sensitive wonder could exist…"

The force of her natural beauty entangled him with silence, his vocabulary dried and his hands trembled.

"Well are you going to say anything back?" laughed Isabel. "You have nothing to be afraid of…"

She had become the imagery of his dreams, the imagery of his verse and the imagery of his prose. She had become all that mattered to him, now becoming immortalized within the contents of his words.

"Talk to her my dear…the affection is mutual…she feels the same way."

As a non interactive personality he was frequently repeatable. If he were to show any emotion, any sensitivity, then it must be done through the vessel of his stage.

"I will write a play!"

A venue deemed illegal and immoral had become an abode to valid inspiration, a canvas to great doubts, great questions, a consolation to his indestructible misery. A genesis shared can become a powerful being, filling the chasms that dwelt within. William had always worn a mask, but now through the disguise of his work he was ready to unveil himself to the world.

"Does he not like me?"

Isabel with her enticing pale skinned complexion had often watched him from afar. Imagining what was, and what could've been. Deepest oceans of blue transfixed onto a mysterious figure that for years had been enchanting her life.

"His silence has nothing to do with you…he's isolated, no one can get too close..."

The two women formed a bond on the characteristics of personality, and through her new friend Isabel learnt all about the man who lived his life behind a veil of words, of impenetrable self. They spoke of poetry, literature, the strokes of Van Gogh, the splashes of Monet; they spoke about History, love and their own aspiring creative ideas. William developed a clearer understanding of his golden haired muse through the various members of his troupe who she had also come to befriend.

"She visits the cellar of Burden, taking in the works of our lost masters," mentioned Charles.

"She has written a book of verse and a novel," exclaimed Annie.

"You're her favourite playwright," mocked Leopold and Stinky laughing and nudging one another.

" Shall I compare thee to a summer's day?" shouted the General with outrage, "Summer's lease hath all too short a date!"

A picture he kept at the forefront of his mind was one of elevated realism, of poetic imagery. The first time he saw her, she eclipsed the darkness that dwelt within their grand surroundings. The artist watched as feelings transcended onto a blank page, pulling open the bud of his deepest thought, his deepest secrets. Whether applauded or ridiculed he needed to purge. He needed to be relieved of this blossoming inferno.

"She'll love it William…I'm sure of it." smiled Annie who encouraged the drafting of his composition.

"You have nothing to worry yourself over."

But The Playwright did have something to fear. He felt that if he were to find happiness, to find bliss, then he could lose his trade, his creativity. For his ideas William needed a bleak history, and a desirous future, dressing in both the darkest and most vibrant of colours. Every outcome hosted something dangerous to his unravelling mortality, his artistic equilibrium.

William had become sick with dread when it came time for the closing monologue. The artist pushing himself past stocks of scenery and piles of props before eventually finding himself back inside the sanctuary of his study.

"What have I done? What have I done!?"

He stood within the yellowed glow of candlelight, enslaved by his own despair, reciting to himself parts of Charles's speech.

"Until now, since the day I first met you…
I have only loved Isabel."

There must be chaos to enable creation. Demons surrounded themselves around Williams's fragile body as they gave strength to the darkest corners of his mind. Clothing themselves in the shadow of anxiety, of self worthlessness. Terror had strangled the air and The Playwright was fighting for breath.

"O' mercy please do not forget me!."

Then he heard it. That marvellous sound, the triumph of applause. The grip loosened around his neck as he found his excelsior, his peace. For that brief moment he no longer cared for Isabel, no longer caring for his isolation, his sorrow. This was the love that he needed. The love of his audience.

"Hear hear," chanted the crowd as the actors bowed before their assembly, stamping their feet in vigorous movement.

William didn't need to be held within the light. Knowing his work had been received, had been enjoyed, had been loved, was all the nourishment he needed. His salvation echoed throughout the room as he stood in silent contemplation. Allowing the present to seep into his memory and deep into his heart. He watched as his work slowly became a portrait of the artist, a portrait of himself. Every narrative contained a seed of truth, blossoming within the space of the painted theatre, allowing him to truly live within the spirit of the performance.

"William?"

There was a knock on the door.

The applause had grown silent and the theatre left empty. The illusion of grandeur quickly becoming lost among the relics of his madness. To reveal himself from the shade, to feel the richness of belonging once more, he knew he would have to create again.

" William may I come in, I'd like to talk to you…"

The Spring Heeled Rhymer

To Inspector Millar he was always the most disturbing, the most ruthless. I never heard a man talk with such malice, with such hate. In his eyes, the spring heeled rhymer epitomized all that was evil. Drenching the skin of a finely tuned society with venomous characteristics, with poisonous ideals.
"Step back…all of you step back!?"
Verse was a dangerous medium. A form which rooted itself within the consciousness of those who submitted to its thoughts, who submitted to its domineering presence.
"I'll tell you again…step back!"
It was a catalyst for expression, an ode to the individual and a force to be reckoned with.
Millar had grown accustomed to art becoming abhorrent to his cold and precise manner. Seeing the work of creation as a plague, a disease of the senses, slowly dismantling the reign of his reality. He could never put himself into the stance of false position, allow himself to become possessed by the words of a stranger or become enchanted by the wonders of a painting. A machine against the manifestation of sensitive emotion, of unifying spirit.
The case absorbed all of his attention, carefully picking out the traits and characteristics of an unravelling personality. Her Majesty's police were aware of his great intellect, his great philosophical and poetic understanding. Who felt a compulsive urge to create. To burden the streets with the mould of an aging formula, an aging bygone relic of the past.
He quoted Byron and Shelley, Wordsworth and Keats, including the treacherous rhythms of his own tongue. He lurked within the darkest shades of colourless London, allowing his seeds to bloom within the heart of Victoria's populous.
Crows feasted upon the dew drenched earth as Inspector Millar made his way into the church yard of St Bartholomew's to discover the poet's latest abomination.
"What does it mean?" asked members of the gathering assembly as he pushed his way through the unwashed Anglican crowd of west Smithfield.
"What does it say?"
And there it was. Another verse neatly scrawled across the wall. Standing in its white chalked uniform, announcing itself to the world. Rain scattered upon the heads of gravestones and the inquisitive congregation, slowly cleansing the holy priory of its insurgent ideal.
"Make sure it washes off completely," ordered the Inspector.
"I want it gone!"
The clouds rewove their sharpened grey as Millar became captive to his

malicious temperament. Scorn filled stares towards the faces of a witnessing rabble, unknowingly clenching his fate within the grip of their hands.

"What does it say?" Shouted a voice strained with agitation. "We want to know!"

The churchyard was held in a regime of silence as a young girl came to the forefront of her audience, and to The Inspector's horror revealed their answer.

"We are many, they are few…"

Eyes looked at one another in bemused contemplation as thoughts tried to dismantle the rhythm of her words, trying to bring meaning to this peculiar spectacle. The black iron gates crashed open as a heavy wind made itself present, while Millar walked through the invading mud to bring a command to one of his young constables.

"I want that young girl arrested, she can read, she's dangerous."

The underlying social constructs of their communities were a finely tuned instrument, construed in a precise ordered and disciplined manner. The mouths of subjects were fed only what didn't make them hungry. They were given gambling and games, breweries and brothels, but nothing that made them rethink their place in society, revaluate their impoverished status. The crowd were dispersed back into their homes and back into the shadows of their vacuous derelicts, humble to the vicious forces that controlled their cultural abstinence.

The spring heeled rhymer was becoming folklore, a modern hero, a man Millar suspected the people were becoming courageously fond of. Tales of their devilish outlaw were scattered across the city in the print of newspapers and in the dialect of conspiring backroom gossip.

Millar understood the psychological pattern of artists. He understood the egotism, the madness behind such a craft. Becoming well versed in the intellectual nourishment of his nemesis.

He had seen the work of grand masters in the ransacking of galleries, in the homes of detained academics. He paid witness to the power these objects possessed over the soul, while crushing their ability to dwell within the carapace of his body.

"Sir… he will see you now."

Anguish palpitated through the skin as the inspector passed through the discoloured corridors of the Black Museum and into the office of Superintendent Anderson. The room was thick with trepidation while quietly being seated in front of his superior's finely furnished desk. Decorated with the medals and ribbons of a celebrated career.

"He's becoming a symbol of disaffection, of a prospering moral turpitude. I want him found Millar; I want him made an example of."

The mind of a detective thrived upon the same stimuli as that of the artist, both reigning in ideas and fragmentations of subconscious to create a picture, to catch a villain. Both obedient to their obsessiveness, both obedient to the drive which fuelled their results.

"I will find him sir, you have my word."

The Inspector sought the same gratification and the same impulse for achievement. Allowing himself to reside in isolation, allowing his thought processes to consistently flow into his work, and into the puzzle of his debauched and potentially ruthless riddle.

Night poured into day as London awoke to its latest scandal. Mist wrapped around the morning air as a new verse unveiled itself to the world. The tenants of Kentish town stared intently at the strange writing laid across Mrs Godwin's wall.

"Rank corruption" shall "pass unheeded by"
Mourning how "Millions to fight compell'd,
To fight or die."

Mud soaked carriages pushed themselves through the barricades of flesh, mesmerised by the potency of dissident words. While officers ran through a slum of destitution, of bleakest indignity.

"There is nothing to see here, move!"

But it was too late. The damage had been done. A line of treachery had been commended to memory, soon to be gathering among the growing whispers of an unvanquishable discontent.

Only a vague description of the spring heeled rhymer had ever been produced. A tall lean figure, who crept within the shadows of the lurid night, woven into the confines of a long black velvet cloak. The streets had become his playground; the streets had become his canvas.

"We need to place harsher regulations on the press. We can no longer allow them to report on this despicable creature's narrative. Send word immediately."

Mush Fakers and flower girls worked the terrain of their filth ridden squalor as The Inspector strolled back to his awaiting carriage. Crawlers endured the bitter cold as a sudden burst of inspiration unveiled to him shards of an uninhabitable light.

Millar had given up every conceived notion, every perceived thought. Allowing a maze of ideas to remould their shape and grace him with a conclusion.

The inspector was able to formulate patterns, to think like a mathematician, to study the relationship between objects, absorb their contents and mould them into a spark of intuition.

The spring heeled Rhymer was a ghost, a spirit brought to life by the influence of a turbulent dead, who could evaporate from the scene of his sickened deed without encountering any human presence. The cast iron Jennings manhole cover had become the source of his latest genesis.

"He's using the sewer system."

Millar waited until nightfall. His stern glare penetrating the physicality of his surroundings. Dissecting every possible outcome, every well conceived manoeuvre, his colleagues watched him with intense scrutiny.

Some thought the operation was a bootless errand. That the spring heeled Rhymer could strike anywhere within the nocturnal domain of their city. That nothing could disclose the future whereabouts' of a ghoulish fiend. An enigma.

There was method to the madness, an imprint of information within the linguistics of a language that could not be penetrated, that could not be understood. Only Millar could interpret the flow of words to create its simple sentence.

A cavalry of footsteps crept into the vile waters of their own putrid stench, slowly splashing against the small waves of their ghastly and infectious excrement. The orange glow from their lanterns broke though the sphere of shadowy brickwork which flowed into a frightful and hostile abyss.

"We'll now split up, stay within your groups and be vigilant. We have drawn out a parameter, based upon the situational pattern of this villain's previous crimes. He is without question going to strike within these boundaries tonight gentleman. Good luck."

A pack of constables circled around The Inspector as they made their way through the periled lair of a daemon. Letting their imagination take them into a place where reality met the horror of their dreams. An engulfing stroke of creativity painted by the subconscious.

Tears of black liquid dripped onto their shoulders as they marched through an underworld of rats and empty liquor bottles, through a maze of vermin that littered their bleakest depths. A few rays of moonlight shone through the empty spaces of miniature iron beams entrenched within the surface.

"He'll come soon, I know it."

The inspector felt the dominant feeling of apprehension, the same beating rhythm of an artist about to meet the gratification of his audience. That pulsating connection of intangible chords between himself and the creation of his own self worth. The inevitable capture of his riddles closing climax.

"Sir, Look!"

Against a page saturated with grime a verse slowly unveiled itself to the soft glow of their lanterns, delicately burning within the sombre dwellings of their maker.

"I rise, so they can rise,
we'll unshackle ourselves from sleep
we'll awake in extravagant wonder
And we'll force our tyrants to weep."
The inspector felt his muscles become gripped with tension, enticed by the chilling air of his opaque labyrinth. Letters reigned high in their thick white stance as Millar followed the marks of scratched chalk further into the unknown.
"Sir wait up…!"
He felt restrained, confined to the present, moving rapidly through an incoherent maze of words. Blake and Shakespeare, Coleridge and Wordsworth, he was close…, he could finally feel the menace of his spirits imposing wrath.
The inspector quickly pulled his gun and immediately pointed the Remington towards an obscure figure stood within the furthest depths of the passageway. A silhouette staring through a gaze of impending damnation, of impending doom.
"Is it me you seek…?"
Loud voices drifted into the reverberated whisper of their intimate surroundings, as Millar took slow steps towards the conclusion of his own enigmatic narrative.
"You are under arrest…surrender yourself immediately and I promise you, you will not be harmed."
A howl of convulsive laughter breached the silence of their unlit inferno as the tongue of a merciful finale was squandered.
"You know you have to kill me Inspector..," vocalized between the hushed tones of a rhymer's sombre chuckle,
"Right here within this feculent pool of impurity, do it…"
The inspectors raised left hand was disturbed by the agitation of the senses, betrayed by his dominating need for answers.
"Ideas are dangerous…, kill me Inspector and I will live on, I will become a revenant. Kill me in public and I will become a martyr. Let me live? And I will sculpt the words of my confinement.
As you choose."
The infectious delivery of the poet gripped the air around him, tightening The Inspector's intrigue. The spring heeled rhymer not only created art, but moulded his life into a form, a composition. Turning his existence into a theatrical performance, an object of his own creation.
"We are not our true selves within the reins of your society; we must be free from our corrupted soul!"
Millar knew he could not keep this man alive; this icon, this symbolic

resistance to power.

The Inspector took his aim.

A shot penetrated a shroud of nothingness before smashing into the silence. The death of a body had become reborn as a growing and corrosive mythology.

Millar had found his narrative's end and was not satisfied. Once again he would have to find a case that would feed his unvanquishable hunger. Create the foundation of his own demoralized self worth.

"What shall we do with the body?" Asked a young officer captivated by their long, tall corpse.

"We'll leave him here and make no record of the incident," ordered a cold and sinister inspector.

"The people will forget him. Or if not, then they will remember him as the man who fled their cause, a cowardly warrior caught up within the relics of academia. He has changed nothing. "

As the hours went by, a new verse, vibrant in its form, unveiled itself to a cruel and colourless world.

The prize-fighter

The Bull's grip tightened around the weight of a ring's knotted rope as he awaited the final blow of his rival, his nemesis…Hercules. A host of jesters and mimes, artists and colourful characters sacrificed themselves having become captivated to the scenery of violence, holding onto the gaze of a brutal and desperate deed. Fists of necessity repeatedly smashed into his flesh, into a mould of muscle that had become confined to a pained and tortured stance. It was the armour of a fighter, the body of deprivation.

Alone upon a bloodied stone slab, The Bull awoke to find himself surrounded by coins, a spectator's pittance, their charity. Tobacco smoke danced within the air, weaving through an odour of sweat and a bitter stench of spilt ale's, relics of a past that had been decorative in his defeat.

Fighting had been widely common in the early part of the nineteenth century and had been left unregulated, brutal and ruthless. Untrained amateurs fought with a fist of iron, with a violent stare, searching for their pay, their opponent's blood.

"You there…you need to go," shouted the landlord standing at the entrance of the cellar, "I need to lock up!"

The fighter lifted himself back into the light, slowly moving through a venue of grime and filth, through a lair of damnation, his stride having suffered the most significant affliction, stumbling into a stranger's blood and trails of broken glass until eventually uncovering his belongings.

"I said you need to go!"

The chill captured The Fighter's wounds as he drifted into the nightly abode of London's streets, past trees bare with winter, past snowflakes which had crept beneath his feet, he saw the strain of moonlight and thought nothing of it. Beauty could no longer exist; it could no longer be felt. Carriages rode in their privileged momentum as street crawlers found their way into the shadows, into the bleakest depths, searching to deprive their hunger, the starvation which fed an intolerable pain. They drank to escape, to dream, to forget the mundane hours awaiting them. Bull pulled from his coat pocket a small bottle of whisky and began to down its entirety, washing away the agony that dwelt within, the pains of an aging physicality. He walked the lonely strand in search of shelter, for a place to lay his wounds. He walked past the church and their empty promises, past the graves of a thousand tales; he walked with unease, directionless, like a swarm of litter scattering across a rough and sleepless domain. Flakes of crisp white brought purity into the hour's embodiment of destitution, cleansing a landscape of a rotting infestation, of its situational personality, Bull saw his chance to act.

Through an open window The Fighter had climbed into a studio that had been tinted with golden candlelight, bruising against hanging canvases and a thick texture of darkness. The art had submerged itself deep within the shadows, as he moved further into the room, contemplating within a bemused and squinted stare.

"What is this place?"

Bull felt every frame did not manifest itself into a true representation, into a true form of reality.

Thick strokes of red rubbed against the harsh blues of a subject's glare, a bruised and hurting manifestation, the painting seemed to be a reflection, fragmentations of The Fighter himself.

"Who's there?" bellowed a voice dwelling within the shade, within the confinements of an unlit corridor.

"Who are you?" A small, frail figure walked into the gallery of his mind, through the imagery of his insufferable and tormented thought, a painter, by the name Franz Derchef.

"What are you doing here?"

The Fighter stood his ground, refusing to move away from the warmth of a medium that perplexed him, that made him feel, somehow relating to a form that had been born out of the imagination, out of creativity; he saw great beauty within this artist's most disturbing work.

"So you like what you see do you?" asked The Painter softening his tone.

"That man was involved in a bar brawl, his image fascinated me." Bull looked upon his host with intrigue, allowing his wounds to burn bright within the orange glow of the fire.

"Oh my, what happened to you?"

The Fighter's swollen knuckles palpitated upon shaking hands, trembling within a newly acquired thought, he stared broken into the gentle eyes of a stranger before being brought with a miraculous offer.

"Allow me to paint you."

The room had become gripped with silence, left with no choice, a stern statement, Bull looked towards the ground contemplating this artist's intention, this mans's reasoning.

"Why would you want to paint me?

The artist moved around the lurid setting of his abode, gathering paints and a stool for his newly found model, his fiercest subject yet.

"To turn something into beauty is what art is, your complexion is encapsulating, your body intriguing, the shell of great pain, you'll make a fine painting, a great piece for my collection." Bull hesitantly pulled himself onto the stool and removed his shirt, allowing his scars to gently mould within the paint, their thick textures engrained within the dirt.

Over a decade Franz had painted many young men to capture their wounds, their essence, to fulfil a vision dreamt within his nightmares, within the screams of a decadent city. The Painter saw something within the misery of sadness, something romantic, an image to be speculated upon, to be immortalized. Something attractive for the darkest spaces of our souls. Over the coming months this ritual took place, and as The Fighter's skin became torn, and battered swollen, the paintings gave him a sense of worth, a sense of some greater meaning, something worthy of his punishment. The crowds cheered in their veracious applause as each new day gave birth to a spectacle of violence, of an evening's entertainment.

"You're my finest subject Bull, I adore painting you."

The two men had struck up a professional relationship, admiring one another's talents, their inwoven existence. Sometimes Franz would make his way into the backrooms of the strand and capture his subject in action, placing small bets amongst his creative and downtrodden friends, always in the hope of making their fortune. The gang leader Mr Wasco had been in attendance, the brain child of this operation, this underground world of fighting, and once a notorious ringmaster of a travelling theatre troupe. It was a setting of debauchery, a place of sinister intention. The streets would always be lonesome in their empty decay, but somewhere The Fighter was loved, he was being admired.

The Music Den

There are places where a man can buy his salvation, his refuge. Thomas made his way down a steep flight of steps before walking into a long low room, decorated with wooden berths and thick with smoke.

"Are you here for music?" asked a pale faced attendant in a low and hoarse voice.

"Please…follow me."

Through the light of a flickering oil-lamp Thomas was taken past rows of strange bodies, pale and unkempt to an empty bunk on the far side of the passage. Bursts of red light glimmered in the gloom as Thomas led himself down and immersed himself in darkness. Out of the shadows he could hear art, the beautiful sound of music.

"For you sir…two shillings."

Graceful notes brought everyone into their own silent contemplation as the attendant put away Thomas's coat and fetched him a pipe.

His mind had already begun to relax as he inhaled the burning poison, a toxic substance that enhanced the sounds around him. Music had become his addiction and the habit grew upon him, more and more he craved the company of this eternal form.

"Thank you," whispered Thomas as he handed back his pipe, closed his eyes and laid back down onto the vile unwashed pillow. Incoherent mumbles from the strangers around him slowly drifted into silence as he became captivated by melody.

The violin strings tightened with sadness as the Chinese attendant made his way back to his chair beside the orange glow of the fire. But through all of their despair, they could all hear the transcending sounds of beauty, the melodies of their space.

Waves of nostalgia were gently crashing against their bodies as the saddest memories became something glorious, something pure. The musicians played from the depths of their souls, and all could feel their invisible touch.

Thomas had been introduced to music two years previous by his friend Clement Moore. an ageing doctor who unveiled to him all that London had to offer. Together they walked through the east end and divulged in the arts, from poetry readings to underground theatre, before eventually finding the gift of music.

"There is nothing more magnificent than of what we just heard," he once said after finding their first den a short walk away from the notorious Gin ally.

"We must go again."

Neither of the two men had felt anything like it. Both agreed that the sounds they heard could be described in human form. Seductive, confident, sometimes bodacious, sometimes shy. It had taken them deep into their subconscious and given them sanctuary, given them escape.

Men from all classes defied the law to find catharsis. Rich and poor laying side by side in their society's perceived debauchery, their perceived evil. "Music touches us where words cannot. It's energy, a universal language, an outburst of love! When sick and weary it brings solace, it brings hope! It unites us, binds us in our darkest night. Human nature cannot do without, music must live! It is literature of the soul, and it must burn bright."

Images projected onto Thomas's eyelids, faces from a forgotten world, a forgotten history. Replaying the memories too painful to bare alone. He held himself still as a warm glow moved through him and penetrated his solitude, his heart.

Those distant words, those distant eyes, a magic binding joy with woe."

He felt the presence of a lost love being reunited with him in song. Chords capturing her spirit, her perfection, her essence. It brought about lost friends and lost dreams. But it also soothed his future, giving him a sense of peace. He could no longer be without music, it filled the places where there was nothing but dread, nothing but emptiness. It gave new breathe to the turbulent winds of his day, and gave them their meaning.

He remained in a state of semi consciousness as the notes brought him further out of his loneliness, and deeper into their realm. He drifted back into childhood, and drifted back into hell. But the day had been cleansed, and the night had been made well. He could live more effortlessly, with this ritual in place.

With his long, pale and skinny complexion Thomas had to make his way to the Dark England often in disguise. He was terrified of being imprisoned, of bringing shame upon the family name, but his addiction was powerful, and it enslaved him. The dungeons of deepest London had become an abode; a sanctuary to the most dominant art form man had produced. Music.

Jacque Burden thoroughly stirred the concoction. Allowing a tincture of extremely bitter laudanum to swiftly dissolve into Ms Whittaker's port. The measurements were precise, the opiate delicately contained.

"Are you aware of Vanbrugh Mr Russo?

Snow danced upon an opaque canvas, elegantly drifting within the bowed windows of Ms Whitaker's luxurious penthouse.

"*The Relapse* is contained within the binding's of my library. I could show you…? If you'd like?

A gothic structure embraced the majesty of high ceilings and tailored interiors, enhancing an individual's sense of place. A scarlet colouring moved through the flickers of gold tinted candlelight, burning within the shade of a nocturnal deception.

"I would like that very much, "grinned Jacque as he took a seat beside the fire. " I've never read his work."

A warm glow melted into the skin of their opulent abode as each conversationalist became bound by a graceful stare, moulding the silence to satisfy their own discreet thoughts.

"My servant Henry will bring the play out to you; an astounding work…a masterpiece. You can read the manuscript before you leave here tonight Mr Russo, it's magnificent!"

Carriages were heard travelling through a blanket of ashen white, while hands on the grandfather clock struck themselves into the untimely hour of midnight.

"It's time to take my leave Mr Russo; I hope you enjoyed your evening. Will I have the pleasure of your company again?"

The chimes of the occasion burst open into the confinement of their rich territory, surrounding themselves with artefacts, once dwelt upon by the gaze of an artistic spirit.

"I'm sure you will Ms Whitaker, goodnight and pleasant dreams."

"Goodnight Mr Russo."

Jacque Burden was tall and lean, an intellectual, a scholar, a gentleman thief. He was stirred by an intoxicating idealism; of a man's inner creation. Moved by the stroke of the brush, by the swipe of the pen, he feasted upon their beauty, their spiritual essence.

"Here you are sir."

A pristine copy of Vanbrugh's *Virtue in danger* was placed delicately in his hands. Jacque slowly unveiled each page, allowing the writer's aging narrative to unravel before his

youthful presence. The words flowed into a tale of a husband and wife and their new temptations, a sequel to Colly Cibber's *The fool in fashion.*

"I'll be taking my rest if there is nothing else you need sir?"Burden read each line with a thorough and concentrated eye. Commending as much as he could to the gallery of his mind, to the collage of his memory.

"That will be all Henry thank you."

Jacque in his theatrical beard, spectacles and top hat, had spent the last six months gaining the trust of his victims. Befriending Elizabeth Whittaker at the painted theatre and using his charismatic nature to draw himself closer. He was a master of manipulation, a master of disguise.

Burden stood up, placing Vanbrugh's book within the inside pocket of his suit jacket. Silent, listening to every creak, every cough, every closing door; waiting for the penthouse to fall to its nightly slumber. He had a plan in place, to enter the library and take the city's most needed treasures, the city's most needed verse.

Jacque didn't believe in private ownership, in private collection. He wanted the complete liberation of art, to be seen before the gaze of anyone with the desire to do so. His cellar had become notorious, holding the creation of ancient masters for all to witness, for all to see.

" Mr Russo; I do not have to be discreet... The hand of the law does not strike at those in positions of privilege, in positions of power. We can do as we like my friend; we can do as we wish...what an honour..."

Burden had much respect for Elizabeth; a strong, independent woman who defied the culture entrenched within her society. She did not love, honour and obey. But instead she forged her own path, one in which she suffered the most extreme ridicule.

Luke Fildes had devoted himself entirely to portraiture within the age of his maturity. A grandson to the political activist Mary Fildes, he had abstracted Ms Whittaker's youth, immortalizing it within the frame of her most prized possession. Long curls of chestnut brown brought out the pale and mesmerizing complexion of his hostess. Lips of pouting red succumbing to the thick black texture of her eyes. The painting hung proudly within the protection of a gold, handcrafted case, staring intently into the conscience of those who dined upon the nourishment of her library.

The time had come to act.

Jacque moved swiftly through the scratched mouths of a groaning wooden floor, through the grit filled chapters of Dante, the enticing verse of Shakespeare. But he was here for something else, something that had been profoundly forgotten.

"I wonder if you can help me?" asked Isabel as she strolled into the cultural sanctity of Burden's cellar. Looking over her left shoulder, in fear of being followed.

"I'm looking for a manuscript?

The cellar was confined to a small room, trapped within a square of pale white brick, littered with the relics of various forbidden forms. Tall structures of verse and prose were piled high while sculpture and pottery presented themselves to a crowd of canvas and enticing illustration. Burden was comforted by a wealthy estate and was able to dedicate his life to the restoration, collection and theft of art.

Through a sailor named Rimbaud, Jacque was able to smuggle in vast quantities of human expression, purchased through friends who had become exiles to neighbouring Paris. Evading the shackles and peril of their own threatened demise.

"It depends on what it is my dear? What is it called?"

Isabel found herself at Burden's cellar almost every week. Carefully dissecting every sentence, every stroke of paint, allowing herself to move undisturbed through a realm of imagination, through a host of dominant thoughts. Allowing each creator to have complete rein over her troublesome heart.

"It's by a 16th century playwright by the name of Henry Chettle, once described as having joined the poets in Elysium I believe. I have been brought to the attention of his play *The Valiant Welchman*; I have no information on the narrative, the intrigue grips me."

Jacque knew that 16th century manuscripts were nearly impossible to find, with many having been destroyed during the great purge of 1885. He made many enquiries until hearing rumours about a vast literary collection, owned by a woman of the name Elizabeth Whittaker.

Burden became a catalyst to his victim's darkest night. Washing the shelves with a glow of molten wax, as he crossed paths with the likes of Thomas Nashe and Anthony Munday, delicately forcing their work into a black velvet bag.

"What wonders we have here tonight madam…What great treasures."

Burden excavated the thinking of Descartes and Seneca, unfolded the landscapes of Beowulf and Homer. Jacque was in awe, tracing his fingertips along volumes of academic study, of beautiful and historical poetry. Great ideas lived once more within the confinements of their leather bound shells.

"What is this?"

He came across Ben Jonson's *Every man in his humour*, focused upon a gentleman named Kno'well who becomes concerned with his son's moral development. Espionage and comedic error enwove between the lines of Wellbred and a merchant named Kitely, who to Jacque became the temporary voices of their fictionalized age.

"Oft sells his reputation at cheap market.

Nor would I, you should melt away your self
In flashing bravery."
Andrea Calmo unveiled himself within the pages of *La Florina*, while William
Gager flourished in the accomplishments of his Latin dramas. Knowledge
filled the horizon of Burden's mind, and he wished to expand his intellect
within Elizabeth's lair, this labyrinth of experience.

Then he found it; the manuscript he had been searching for, The *Valiant
Welchman.*
"Thank you so much Mr Burden," smiled Isabel as he handed her an antique
booklet,
"I will begin reading it immediately!."
Jacque was proud of his profession. He was a liberator of art, a liberator of the
soul, who allowed the spirit of the dead to move through the heart of the
living, to remain within the lineage of their history.
"There is one more thing Mr Burden. I have recently become engaged to the
playwright William Caswell; we hope to start a new life together in Paris. I
thought your friend Rimbaud might help us?"

The Dandy

Thomas belonged to the cult of self. A man who placed particular importance on appearance, a refined and elegant use of language, and his sport. A gallant who cared for nothing except to satisfy his own passion, his own wicked desire.
"Come out and play my friends….I'm waiting."
A defined aesthetic, an impulsive eccentricity, Thomas pursued the creatures of the night with style, with perpetual wit.
"I will not be bound to your chains Sir… I will not be your prisoner"
Snow invaded the rapturous shadows of Bethnal Green, lurking beneath the finely polished shoes of a vigilante, of a heartless fiend. A typical outfit consisted of a black woollen tailcoat and a large bow tied cravat. To his enemies Thomas had become known as The Dandy.

A tight leather glove clutched a long tasseled walking stick, as his slim figure moved closer towards his nemesis, his prize. A silhouette striding through their opaque street, furnished with a pocket watch and an immaculate fur plush top hat. Thomas was possessed by the hour of the hunt, by the hour of the chase.
Fear had deeply sunken into the outlaw's flesh, limbs pulsating against the swollen air and the presence of faceless obscurity. A scream bellowed from the anguished harlot's mouth.
"AAAARGGGGGG…"

Through a battalion of ashen white, a plume of fire pushed the dandy back. A stream of fuel having jumped from the performer's violent and pallid lips. Fredrick had once been known as The Dragon's Breath, an infamous fire breather. His grand talent illuminating his heavily scarred and bold complexion, while patchy makeup displayed his theatrical past. A man filled with venom, a man consumed by hate.
"And now I know which one you are!" grinned Thomas in a playful and sinister manner. "This is going to be easier than I thought."
He was up against an opponent heavy in their stature, fearful in their gaze, dressed in a finely tailored scarlet robe, worn from the degradation of poverty, from unwarranted infliction. The heat of venom came once more, as the performer commanded his obedient reign of energy, a harmful and skilled inferno. Intense heat bruised against the dandy's skin as he elegantly slipped past the vehemence of Fredrick's ruthless strike.

"Well that was close," he muttered as he took back his insolent position, directly in front of his rival. "Would you like to try again?"

A heavy gust of wind brought in a maelstrom of snowflakes, blinding the breather, and becoming a veil that revealed itself as the hunter's natural accomplice. The Dandy moved quickly, swiping his cane violently against the thick chill of their darkened air, moving forwards with courage and at a rapid pace.

The Dragons Breath retreated back into the shadows, back into the darkest shade of London's filthiest squalor, becoming invisible to the nocturnal empire surrounding Thomas's sight.

"You can't hide forever you freak, reveal yourself to me you coward!"

The game had started some years previous and was yet to find a conclusion. Art in all forms was conflicting within the structure of established thought, within a governing and vacuous orthodoxy. Circuses were disbanded, leaving performers with nowhere to go, without love nor occupation. Their strange characteristics, their ugliness, their introverted personality drove them into the darkness. Becoming bound to an unfair narrative, conceptualized by many as ghoulish monsters, haunting the majesty of a finely construed society. Seen as unwanted relics of a forbidden and treacherous past.

They had been the kindest; gentlest seeds buried within existence, and like Frankenstein's monster had grown angry at the world, souls becoming inwoven into the fabric of bitterness, into the traits of reigning malice. The Dandy didn't care for their deeds, what was legal and what was not. To him this was a desirable activity, a sport which combined mental as well as psychical nourishment. He was transfixed upon the chase, transfixed upon his achievements.

Thomas was also a writer, and under a false pseudonym wrote countless verse and essays based upon visiting the notorious music dens which littered his city. Visiting underground theatre, the wondrous visualization of paintings. He was a man who wanted to cultivate beauty and mould his life into a form of adorned fabrication.

"Why do you seek me? Why do you wish to bring about a violent end...?"

Under the disguise of night, Thomas divulged within the flamboyancy of London's theatrical underworld. He fought knife throwers and a menacing troupe of disturbed gymnasts, a delinquent set of clowns, before confronting a notorious ringleader of the name Pierrot.

"Come out; come out where ever you are..."

The Dandy's name grew infamous after his capture of the fugitive John Merrick, a name transformed into that of the elephant man, one of his proudest and most acclaimed achievements.

"You're just a piece of meat, why don't you reveal yourself? So we can settle this more efficiently hmm..?"

Then he smelt it. The smell of kerosene, the catalyst of Fredrick's violent and most dangerous act. His body was submerged in nothingness, alone within the wide abyss, but he felt it, he could feel the breather's presence.

"You're close my friend, you're very close indeed..."

Instantly their surroundings became illuminated, the fierce glow from a flame was spat towards the paleness of the nightly sky, and burnt with decadence, with venomous defiance. The Dandy moved quickly, once again swiping his cane towards his nemesis, swiftly moving around each confluence of fire and sweltering resentment that had been sent towards his persistent stride.

"Take that you swine!"

There was a howl of pain. Fredrick slumped down towards his bloody knee, clenching a pulsating wound cast upon him by a deadly foe. Thomas stood above him with a smile, his cane placed gently back against the hard, cobbled path.

"It seems I have won my friend? Any last requests?"

Death lingered within his words, unbound from the tongue, his villain's downfall agonized against a canvas of crisp white. Tears of terror eclipsed Fredrick's emotion as he slowly pushed himself back from his inevitable fate.

"What do you want!?"

Fredrick was the last name on Thomas's list. In six months the Dandy had taken down the entirety of Mr Wasco's theatre troupe, a deed in which he would receive no credit.

"There he is, there he is
There he is once more,
its Leopold the clown
He entertains the poor

He stands upon a rooftop
He plays a violin
And in the act of being naughty
He makes us laugh and sing."

This children's nursery rhyme had caught his attention, a mythical creature that lived within verse.

As a young man, Thomas Atley was once a great and highly respected adventurer. He trekked through the Himalayan regions, looking for the Yeti, through the forests of North America looking for Bigfoot. A man suffering from sickness, from the psychotic necessity of game hunting, whether man or animal.

Leopold the Clown

To us he was a mystery. A mythical creature of the night.
For a crowd with a finely adjusted temperament he brought distraction, he brought beauty. Allowing his audience to indulge in a delicate and softer passion.
Above the narrow streets of St Gile's, I witnessed him for the first time. Holding the hand of my mother as we made our way through the ghastly labyrinth of blackened brick surroundings. Through the thick grey colours of smoke and soot, and mud that drowned our feet.
Cracked windows littered this putrid canyon of despair, this soul destroying slum of unvanquishable poverty. Lanterns crept into the darkness as we looked up towards the dominant full moon and his brightest star.
Above a tenement building stood the man himself Leopold.
Eyes watched him greedily as tenants made their way into the narrow maze of Old Nicol, to catch a glimpse of this strange figure.
"Who is that Mummy?" I asked with amazement as she clenched my hand tighter, keeping me still as a crowd moved past us, skirting pools of filthy liquid.
"Who is that man?"
The sun had been leached away but Leopold always brought with him her aura, her presence. Smiles crossed my face each time I saw him bring joy back through a veil of unwashed madness. Laughter blossomed throughout the assembly as we watched him juggle and dance and display his magic, while shedding a tear when he performed a variety of tender emotions.

Love and loss became entwined with life and death as the rooftop became his stage, a mime expressing the beauty of a flower unknown to our thoughts. He was sometimes accompanied by a range of beautiful sounds hosted by an antique violin, letting the waves of his heart travel into the deepest seas of our own.
He was mystical, a dream captured by the confinements of reality.
"I hope to see him again too my dear...we'll keep our eyes open for him."
That very day he became the imagery of my sleep, the subject of my mind. His worn down brown suit, patchy clown makeup and large top hat became a caricature of escape. His sweetest emotions were somewhat lost upon me as a nine year old girl, but his silliness allowed me to witness happiness, to witness amusement.

Every full moon Leopold returned to the rotting terrace house and the crowds would gather merrily beneath him. Applause slapped against the cold and putrid air at every performance, as Leopold bowed before his pilgrims with graciousness and with pride.

We never heard his voice…Leopold being only a name laid upon him by a loyal audience. A man with no history, with no future, an icon of the present, and a spark within the abyss.

"We love you!" people would shout from the depths below, for although he was a stranger to them, they felt an understanding, Leopold's life having transcended through his art, feeling a genuine connection with him.

He performed his dance, he sometimes dressed up, every show was different, and every show a spectacle. Word of mouth brought more and more into the moonlit streets of Bethnal Green to witness this new wonder.

Families marched past the carcasses of dead cats and dogs, passed the various obscenities of destitution, to reach divinity, to find a sanctuary from their hell. Leopold fuelled my child's imagination, my creativity. I would gather with my friends in the damp squalor of our homes and together we would take turns performing for one another, miming and dancing, pretending to be our hero. We made up stories about him, chalked his picture into the walls with stone, we worshipped him. Then one day, without warning he disappeared, becoming exiled from our loving, admiring gaze. His audience had elevated him into myth. Leopold was a man I could never forget…

Isabel's Diary

In nineteenth century France, there lived a man, considered to be one of the most talented personages of artistry and showmanship. His name was the Magnificent Burden, the most celebrated illusionist of his era. Gifts and ambition were restricted to his domain, to perform the greatest tricks mankind had produced, to leave an audience spellbound. In later years Jacque would become a confidant and friend, a gentleman thief. A man who dedicated his life to the collection and preservation of a forbidden form, a vessel to the revenant of art.

To our content he would captivate the world once more, with a miraculous escape. William and I were sat at breakfast in the Montmartre district of Paris when we received word of his inexplicable feat, this grand statement of defiance. From London's Dark Tower, Burden had vanished from the confines of his cell, leaving no trace of his method.

"What pleasant news," smiled William as he read the morning paper, "a fine gentleman."

 The narrative had become a sensation, a feast for the imagination, captivating headlines for many months to come.

We often walked through the galleries of our much beloved abode, past street performers and portrait artists, peering through book shops, in awe of this colourful and vibrant landscape. We could see the composure and characteristics of a joyous existence, of a free soul. I was in the sanctity of creativity, and in the refuge of knowledge.

With Jacque's help we had been able to sail the darkened tide to our exile, the waves to a new beginning. He was a stalwart, a man who could never be forgotten.

The flow of the pen always returned to the darkest part of my subconscious, my past. England haunted my salvation, and dwelt within my verse. Would I ever be free? Free from this turbulent vacuous dream.

Exile

We sailed upon the darkest waves
As tides glittered white
Alone upon the wide abyss
In the frost and chill of night

We were destined for Paris
To find a sanctity for art
And upon Rimbaud's aging ship
A vision ached my heart

Of all the lost faces
Brothers, sisters and friends
Who we'd left behind
In the shadows of the end

Of the tall dark towers
Menacing in their reign
Above a sky of darkest grey
My visions lucid flame

London

I sit from afar, over a glittering sea,
From bitter, sterile mortality
A garment adorned to shroud the night
O' London, now eclipsed by the night

A bud pulled open the darkest ground
To find the birth to be
Seeds enrich the baron land
As corruption impelled us to flee

Hidden faces mould the rhyme
Imprison a trail of thought
Who kept the shape of a vacuous reign
But with words like weapons, we thought

It was transcendent upon the tongue
And aggressive against the ear
Even with humour, dance and song
The establishments eyes, drenched fear.

Williams Dog

The maddened dog loosened his grip
Before ripping him from his flesh
In his stare a punctured face
Bruising with blood as flowers thresh

Carved then branded with fire
He twist and turned once more
Growling against the daylight
And his suffering voice at war

Frail hours bound the day
As he tore him limb from limb
Descending into nothingness
Clenching bloodied skin

Stretched in bones he widened
The bellow of man had strayed
The fortunate love had withered
In a battered tomb he laid

He dragged him down to misery
He dragged him down to hell
Upon a cursed and swollen heart
He let his sorrow dwell

Beneath the Painting

I have spread softly beneath your dreams
Enwrought my comforting light
A naked mind, its clothes are worn
Rests against a foreboding night

I nursed a transfixed moon
And sailed a bitter sea
Passing by my heart's agony
And the emptiness to be

We should hide from life's gaze
To find a beauty in our eyes
Alone among the pale clouds
And the singing lullaby

I celebrate the life that's long
Under a darkened wind filled sky
And praise the departing ghost of sleep
And the moments when the soul does cry

The devilish murder of the head
Bids the tongue farewell
For they have planned their neurotic deed
And the day has been made unwell

But I protect the dangerous past
And the sorrowful mourning sound
For I may not be
Like our nature, paving the ground.

Stinky

There's Stinky, there he is again
The bigmouth we adore
A dwarf clown with the biggest smile
And the stench from being poor

There's stinky, there he is again
A picture in my mind
Mischievous, devilish, but charming
Horrible, cunning, but kind

There's stinky, there he is again
In the ruins of the night
With his friend Leopold
Searching for the light.

The General

"This life, which had been the tomb of his virtue and of his honour."
The General bellowed from the confinement of his madness, twisting and
turning within the shackles of his imprisonment, within the chained scream of
an invented illusion.
He sat within the depths of his cell with three close friends, Macbeth, King
Lear and Hamlet. Beneath the world they were graced by walls of bare stone,
half lit by a dangling naked light in the centre of the room.
"Come not between the dragon and his wrath," smiled Lear, pleading for him
to continue.
The filthy squalor of The General's incarcerated body produced a repugnant
odour, a putrid stench, a smell of fear. Toothless, pale creatures stood within
the shadow of bedlam's corridors, within the hallway of insanity's night.
"Oh I suffered with those that I saw suffer."
Visions plagued his existence. Only the theatre had given him sanctuary, his
solace. He had lived to perform, to entertain. To bring sadness, joy, laughter,
to bring his characters and their turbulent worlds to life.
Slumped down, wearing a waistcoat which proudly displayed his ribbons, The
General stared at his three friends intently.

"Which many a good tall fellow had destroy'd
So cowardly; and but for these vile guns
He would himself have been a soldier."

The General expressed himself through the tongue of Shakespeare, through
the beauty, the sadness of his much beloved dialect, his much beloved verse.
He was haunted by the memories of war, the imagery of bloodied flesh. Limbs
hung from bare trees, while death rattled consistently through his cell door;
life for him had become an unquenchable agony.
"A poor player, that struts and frets his hour upon the stage, and then is heard
no more."
The asylum was filled with creative intellect, with magnificent talent. Reasons
for admission into Bedlam during the reign of Victoria consisted of many,
egotism, hard study, grief, to be creative. The General's withdrawal from
reality had spared him his life, sparing him the misfortune awaiting some of
his closest friends, his family.
It was a place that held the city's most disturbed psyche, but Bedlam could be
no more insane than those who held power, who reigned over this
manifestation of corrupted establishment. Their madness was a reflection of
the times, their asylum a prison where the incurable could be swept from sight,

from acceptance. Their confinements riddled with scandal, patients dying from having been chained to confined spaces, others forced to sleep naked, tormented by sadistic keepers. The bottom windows were unglazed and the cells were exposed to the coldest air, leaving the basement galleries damp. The patients were severely underfed, pale thin victims of an abhorrent government, of an intolerant system, forever kept within the shackles of their burdening mentality.

"Make mad the guilty, and appal the free."

The General and his three friends were quite fond of the many characters that lurked within the spaces of their miserable dwellings, within the chamber of their despair. Two cells down from The General, was a man who had become known as The Watchmaker. He was an elderly gentleman, a man obsessed with the past, obsessed with the imagery of a bygone love, a man who held no desire for the present.

For years he had locked himself away within his lavishly constructed workroom, setting the hands on his elegantly crafted clocks to the hours of personal significance,

"Memories are what we are; we are always bound to what has been."

There was a man with a constant need to hear music, a woman who felt a constant need to document her life, developing the name The Collector. There was Orthello the contortionist, Fredrick the psychic, all of them seeds that had been kept from their blossom, from their beautiful and theatrical fate, their destiny.

"A friend should bear his friend's infirmities." smiled Macbeth towards his troubled confidant.

"I count myself in nothing else so happy, as in a soul remembering my good friends," replied The General, unknowing whether his nightmare would ever come to an end.

The Painter

Someone must have tempted Franz into this way of thinking. For without having done anything wrong, he had himself declared fit for death one beautiful winter's morning. Slim and carrying himself in a fine fitting suit, only his aging landlady wept as he was given his sentence. "Your purpose will be served," said the judge, "your sacrifice will be granted." The room had become electrified in conversation as Franz studied his executioner with silent intensity. He had allowed himself to be submitted to a cruel and critical examination, one which brought the vilest remarks and utmost scrutiny towards his very existence.

"Is there anything you'd like to say?" questioned the judge.

"No," replied Franz.

Crowds of whispers began to bind themselves together, strangers twisting and turning in awe of their judgement. The room had become wrapped in a veil of darkness as little light could push past the dusty lattice window, a sinister place that had become lost to a cruel and colourless world. There was a knock on the door. A man stepped in whom Franz had never seen before. Furnished with pockets, buckles, chains and an officer's attire, the man made his way through the court's audience to Franz's side at the dock.

"This is Commissioner Joseph Kramer," explained the judge.

As a painter, Franz had allowed many gentlemen to sit for him, but none affected him like the presence of a handsome Lord Douglas, the man he desired, the man he loved. For weeks, the two men worked together, to capture his essence, this man's gift to life.

All beautiful forms eclipsed what should've been a stroke of light, imposing misery where happiness should dwell. Douglas's had brought an unquenchable agony, a beauteous thirst for more, a painful impossibility. Life for him had become empty; a struggle, a narrative he no longer wished to take to its natural conclusion. Franz was finally ready to confront the mercy being gripped by the impendence of his death, the finale, to this terrible, abhorrent dream.

"Without love life is worth nothing, to be alone is just to exist."

Thoughts were rapidly pulsating through his mind, silent images flickering through a life of imperfection, through a collage of worthlessness. The isolation from childhood strengthened as he progressed into old age, no great finale, no beautiful ending could now possibly be awaiting him. All his trials, his defied expectations were never to be greeted with reward, no richness to sooth the projection being carried out by his weary eyes. The Painter had been swallowed up by self pity, flesh bitter wrapt around a frail, ungrateful frame, smothered in a deceived and uncomfortable ugliness. Franz's portraits captured the torture of his mind's landscape. Strokes of dark colour and harsh swipes distorted the angelic quality of the subject, transferring pain into a tangible and potentially celebrated piece. Something he could be proud of, a reason to suffer.

He had been in a grand opaque courtroom surrounded by the faces of those who he had once been acquainted, friends, lovers, enemies. Smiles and sinister scorns decorated the audience's expression as Franz bowed his head for the judge to conduct the trial's opening statement.

"We are here today to make a judgement on this man's life. You will all be called to the witness stand accordingly, Mrs Hall, if you would like to go first…"

Emma had once been Franz's fiancée, his solace, the woman who had broken his heart.

" I never loved him, never have, never will, I'm grateful to have him out of my life.".

"Mr Davies,"

"I knew him when we briefly collaborated on an artwork; the man had absolutely no talent, an amateur at best."

"Lord Douglas"

Alfred climbed up towards the witness box and stared towards the defendant with intensity, with venom. Franz's soul was awaiting its murder with only a few simple phrases, a few poison tipped words. He knew what was about to be.

"Yes I admired some of his work, but I could do without it, and could do without his company, he was merely an acquaintance who wanted me to sit for him, that is all." Franz had already realized the outcome, the conclusion to his trial. He stood quietly as many more took to the stand to declare their hatred, their dislike, their indifference. They spoke about his poverty, his occupation, his insecurity; it was all too much to take. So much disgust for a man who only tried to love, to be accepting, now to be pushed away by those closest to him.

"I have made my decision," said the Judge.

"The defendant is guilty as charged."

The courtroom exploded with applause, having received the outcome they all wanted, they all needed. Franz looked towards the ground with a faint smile; He knew it would all be over soon.

Franz awoke back in his quarters at Mrs Smith's squalid South London residence. He was staring out of the dirty lattice window and into the darkness of London's darkest night. Faint within the reflection of the glass he could see the stare of Commissioner Joseph Kramer. He had made his decision; he knew what he had to do.

Sunlight swept across the damp wooden floor as Franz pulled on his shirt and tie and walked towards the window. Aging cleaners swept the streets outside as he checked the time on his pocket watch and applied his waistcoat. There was a knock on the door.

"Mr Derchef?"

"Come on in Mrs Smith," beckoned Franz with invitation.

"Hello Mr Derchef,"

Franz's elderly landlady walked into a room painted with decay. Cracked walls, broken mirrors and mouse droppings were a burden for each of Mrs Smith's tenants. "I was just wondering if you'd like breakfast today?"

"Not today, I have a taxi picking me up outside in a few Minutes, I better hurry."

"Is it concerning your employment?"

" Yes , yes it is," replied The Painter as he combed his hair intently in a nearby mirror, " It's for a very important client."

"Oh my, well I hope it goes well for you."

The gentle sound of a nearby train went by as Mrs Smith smiled and bid her farewells to the tenant as he threw on his raincoat and gloves and saw her to the door.

"Goodbye Mrs Smith," he smiled as he locked the door behind him and made his way down the empty staircase. Drinkers murmured and whispered in their shadows as The Painter made his way into the dirty lobby and out onto the street.

"Where is it you'd like to go?" asked the driver as Franz got into the back of an awaiting carriage.

"The Black Museum"

The air was entwined with a thick fog as the carriage rolled through London's littered streets. Making their way past an endless line of factories, mechanically blowing out smoke into the purity of their sky, burdening its beauty. A canvas of white was being viciously evaporated.

He knew that this is what he had to do, for his name to matter, for his life to have meaning. He would kill the sworn enemy of his love, his tormenter, his muse, the notorious Inspector Millar. Franz had acquired the Remington some time ago, and his intentions were not to murder another, but himself. For hours he stared into the void, placing the gun against the sweat of his temple, revisiting the day of his trial, all the loss, the hate, but somehow unable to define his own conclusion. Somehow unable to carry out his sentence, he would need it forced upon him. He would need the arm of the law and their murderous oppression, to unknowingly help him in his final wish.

Alfred had often spoken of his disgust for Millar, a man who had helped to imprison many of his friends, many of art's greatest talents. If he was to go, he wanted to take The Inspector with him. Franz thought by doing so he would be seen as a martyr, a hero, that he would finally be appreciated, finally be loved. That his art would suddenly become adored, become held in high regard, delusions had completely taken over his body, his heart and his mind, Franz had become a prisoner to insanity.

"Here we are!" shouted the driver.

Franz quietly paid and gave his thanks before crossing the street and strolling into a nearby brewery. The Painter needed a few shots of whisky to calm his nerves and the thoughts beginning to process with panic, with doom. His hand shook violently as he lifted the glass to his lips, and savoured the taste.

"Are you ok Sir?" asked the barman gently as he poured another scotch. "You don't look to good."

Franz ignored this converse of kindness and instead drifted into the future, imagining what could be, The Painter had no time to lose.

He found his position, gently placing his finger over the trigger hidden within his left trouser pocket. Deep breaths were being pushed out through his lungs and into the cold, bitter air.

"What would Alfred think? Would he be pleased? Would he remember me?" Officers marched out through the grand doors of this bleak, discoloured fortress, the headquarters of her Majesty's Police, the home of Inspector Millar. The building had a terrifying presence, a symbol of an oppressive, intolerable regime.

And there he was.

The authority of this tall and lean figure gathered an intoxicating aura as the inspector galloped down the marble steps and towards an awaiting carriage. The Painter had to act imminently. Franz swiftly pulled the Remington from his trouser pocket and moved with force, pushing through the crowd towards his target, his nemesis. Taking in all the pain, all the betrayal gathered throughout his life, giving him the strength to carry out this murderous and brutal deed.

"Millar!"

Before The Inspector could even turn to greet this aging assassin, two shots were fired directly into his spine, spreading streaks of thick red blood across vast flakes of white, as a body slumped down onto the cold and ice ridden road.

Crowds gathered and stared intently towards this predator, this vicious killer. The pistol fell to the ground as Franz bowed his head, and awaited his fate.

Mr Wasco

Jean Wasco had been born on the muddy banks of a fetid odour, of a rippling and darkened Seine. A downpour slapped against his smooth newborn flesh as he was gently placed in a warm, knitted blanket. As an only child he accompanied his theatrical parents across Europe as part of a travelling circus, bringing joy and admiration to thousands across the continent. A life they cherished, a life they desired. As he grew to become a small, stocky and moustached man, the apprentice came to master each and every performance, each and every trade, succumbing to a fierce and broadening intellect. An extraordinary and mesmerizing talent. It wasn't long before he would begin a journey back to England and with some financial backing create his own magnificent spectacle "Mr Wasco's travelling extravaganza."
"This is one of the finest shows the country has ever seen, you should be proud of your achievements."
But it wasn't to last, it wasn't to be.
The British Establishment had instigated a vicious crackdown on all forms of entertainment, of showmanship, pushing them into London's most putrid districts, into a city's bleak and sinister underworld. With everything the troupe owned having been taken from them, it began with petty crime before expanding into gambling, extortion and eventually murder. Fredrick was Mr Wasco's most prominent and most deadly assassin, a man known among various crime syndicates as The Dragons Breath.
"You're the only one I truly trust Fredrick, your loyalty and honour mean much to me."
Each member of this sinister band had grown angry and venomous, their morality lost to the confinements of their past, within the spaces of a bygone hour. Made up of only five performers, Mr Wasco's troupe ruled with an iron fist, becoming the most theatrical, most powerful and feared organized crime gang in London.
"It's all ours my friends…all ours."
With a plush top hat and tailored suit, Mr Wasco would often attend fights run within the cellar of an underground burlesque club, an establishment of many held within his possession.
"That man …Bull, he could be useful to us, I've never seen anyone move like him…I'll be watching this one closely."
Pierrot was Jean's nemesis, his competitor, a rival who held within his grasp performers with a peculiar set of skills, a vicious criminality. Both pale faced masterminds who held a theatrical and egotistical flare, men whose troupes would both come to an abrupt and bloodied end. Mr Wasco composed a list of how each of his accomplices had met their fate, their demise.

Fredrick the fire breather – multiple stab wounds
Amias the whip cracker – drowned
Lindsey the trampeze - fell
Damian the knife thrower – strangled
Gerd the lion tamer – eaten
The strength of his power had been taken from him, murdered in the gaze of a notorious vigilante known as The Dandy. Both ringmasters's had no choice but to force themselves into hiding, to plan a resurgence, their revenge. Mr Wasco had the plan and the means to carry out what could potentially become the biggest heist of the century, to steal from the Bank of England.
"I'm sorry Sir but you're mad, this whole situation is absurd."
Cigar smoked drifted within the confinements of the ringmaster's office, situated within the remains of an abandoned and ash ridden theatre. Eleven new eyes looked upon their employer with bewilderment, with trepidation.
"The plan is full proof, each of you holds a reason for your presence, possessing something I need to make this work, you've been hand picked… and the rewards will be great. Each of the performers looked at one another in silent contemplation, drifting within the fear of excitement, of implausibility. The plan was complicated, intricate and well thought, but they'd have to wait for the right hour in which to strike, to fulfil this grand and perilous undertaking.
On the 18th of February the troupe received what they had been waiting for, the day they had feared. Fires swept across their nightly city as it moulded itself into a landscape of civil war, into the barricades of emancipation. The great uprising. Cavalries charged through proletariat brigades, through a swarm of violent discontent as Mr Wasco gave his order.
"It's time my friends…let us begin."
The Ringmaster stared into a world where minds had bound together and grown into a destructive smile. As the populous strove for a new narrative, a new beginning, one that would eventually be quashed.
"You have been the most perfect of gifts, a spectacular distraction."
Mr Wasco followed trails of illegal thought, visualizing his plan to the exact second, to its precise detail. His troupe would profit within the hours of a long and bitter struggle, within the hours of immense courage. Thousands of prisoners had been liberated from the confinements of their hell, from the solitude of their torture, branded as free men, returning to a cage of illegal notion, to a fearful present. A day that will never be forgotten. The outlaws had been magnificent in their conduction of the robbery, delivering a beautiful and bewildering spectacle in itself. Christoph swiftly moved across his highwire from a neighbouring building, taking out two guards and stealthily making his way to the ground floor, as Robert the Trampze followed in his

pursuit, keeping watch from the rooftop. Joshua rode from within the imagery of dreams, riding through the heat of a city's inferno, a city's crowded plea for salvation. Using his carriage to transport the loot while Lynch and Rebecca (Knife throwers) were left to enter the main façade of the building and make their way into the vault, their prize.

Mr Wasco would soon recapture his empire, once again becoming lord of London's dark and sinister underworld.

The Magician

In his native France, the Magnificent Burden had become a controversial and celebrated performer. Through a series of jailbreaks the magician had found celebrity, wealth and a reputation as an elusive Frenchmen, a brilliant escapologist. A man who the authorities would soon come to scrutinize, fear and investigate, wishing to uncover the secrets of his undisclosed method. While on tour, Burden had been placed in a pair of regulation handcuffs by a police Chief of the name Serge Geynes, an act that would become the catalyst to a series of legendary triumphs.

"I do not know how you do it young man, it is beyond comprehension, without words."

He had escaped with such confidence, with such speed it had left the commissioner amazed, and through hundreds of letters the magician's reputation grew further. Spreading swiftly into the gossiping contemplation of thousands.

"We need to try something new my friend, I'm contemplating the idea of a jailbreak."

Burden was marched to his cell, stripped of his clothes and thoroughly searched. The door was triple locked and his clothes placed in an adjoining room which was then double locked. At The Magicians request, the heavy iron Gate at the end of the corridor was secured with a seven – lever bolt. The odds were against him, but to everyone's surprise he joined his captors a mere three minutes later.

"That's astounding!"

Within that time Burden had managed to get out of his cell, retrieve his clothes and burst through the iron entrance of his confinement. Authoritarian spectators were his only witness to this groundbreaking and mesmerizing performance.

"I have never seen anything like it."

The Magician recreated this stunt throughout the country. In Calais, he escaped from four sets of handcuffs before leaving his cell and scaling the prison wall, only to be found two days later at his residence in Paris. In Marseille, he had even reshuffled the prisoners before evaporating from their secure, cold and sombre dwellings. Whenever possible Burden would test the locks with his key, hidden beneath his hair and held down with a dab of adhesive wax. At other times in his possession was a pair of hollow heeled slippers which swivelled open by pressing a catch. The Magician was a man of many talents; of many disguises.

Burden was a master illusionist, a master of transformation, notorious for a trick in which he could change the characteristics of his own face, letting it mould into the form of a devilish, supernatural creature. Hundreds of gasps would burst open amongst the rich surroundings of the country's theatres, horrifying his audience in ways no one had done so before.

"You did well today Jacque, you should be proud of yourself."

Elizabeth had once been his faithful, loving and confident assistant, the only woman to have ever captured his heart, his true self. Together they devised new tricks, new sources of intrigue, new ways to gather the audience's contemplation, their wonder.

"I don't know what I would do without you, your smile, and your strength."

As companions they were flooded with public interest, hounded by reporters, admirers, those who wished to discover their secrets, their methods. It was all too much to take for two sensitive, troubled and creative souls. They decided to flee to the countryside, but unbeknownst to them, it would be the beginning of a nightmare, the beginning of their doom.

"We'll be ok Jacque, we'll have some peace, no one is going to follow us out here."

With the widespread acclaim the magnificent Burden held, he was beginning to draw unwanted attention from various religious authorities, from various spiritual leaders, convinced that this great conjuror, this great magician was the devil himself.

"This man is dangerous…something needs to be done!"

Then one night Jacque Burden's life would be changed forever. A religious cult had secretly tracked them to their isolated cottage situated on the outskirts of Paris with the intention of killing both husband and wife in their sleep, in their dreams.

But that wasn't to be.

Jacque was touring when he received word of his beloved's demise, carried in the heavy weeps and panting breaths of a surviving servant, who had witnessed this wicked ordeal, this monstrous narrative.

"I'm sorry Jacque, I'm so sorry."

Burden was left distraught; a subject now found within the confinements of hell, within an immense agony, he no longer wanted to be.

Without any conclusion, without any farewell, the Magnificent Burden disappeared, never to be seen again.

The Camp at Dover

The Dandy's horse charged through a landscape of darkened green, in his pursuit of the Odyssey, in the pursuit of his master's prey. Willingly pushing past an insurgence of thick mud as its shards smashed into the cold morning air, sprinting towards a pale and sombre light. The sails of Rimbaud's aging ship rippled viciously as they caught themselves within a heavy wind that swept across the channel, smashing them against tides which rapidly climbed onto the deck.

"I see him; he's at the cliff edge."

Through his battered telescope the captain had caught sight of their pursuer, this menacing and strange figure, moving with speed upon a galloping skin of chalked white.

"Going to the camp is too dangerous; we should change course."

The seeds looked towards their superior with defiance, with hostility. Rimbaud knew with a decision like this he could have a mutiny on his hands. The troupe were immensely loyal to one another, brave and courageous.

"Once more unto the breach!" bellowed The General, "There is special providence in the fall of a sparrow."

The crew nodded in agreement.

After the death of Inspector Millar, London's streets had become submerged in a wave of tyranny, in a wave of murderous oppression. The establishment wanted revenge, and they sought it with blood, with persecution, but instead created a barricade of defiance, a valiant rebellion. In the late hours of February 18th, a crowd of thousands gathered and stormed the dark tower and the gates at Bedlam, the beginnings of an historic event that would come to be known as "The Great Uprising." Mass outbreaks of civil disobedience struck all over the country, with streets swept up within the flames of idealistic unrest, fires burning beneath a nightly sky, and among the charging battles of civil war. An island held within a reign of chaos, within the arena of change. Rimbaud kept watch as the Dandy drifted into the distance, unable to keep up with the fuel that had been captured by their sails and swiftly propelled them forwards.

"We'll go to the camp but we have to be quick, all of us are lucky to have escaped, to have found each other again, I don't want to go back to prison."

The camp at Dover had now existed for sometime, made up of impoverished performers, writers and artists, unable to pay for a passage that could take them to the sanctity of France, to their land of expression. The occupants suffered the most extreme impoverishment, the most extreme hardship, kept alive only by hope, by conviction, that they would one day make it to their refuge.

"When I'm in Paris I'll spend every hour God has given me creating...every hour."

The crew arrived and immersed themselves deep within the crowd, make shift tents were scattered across the rough terrain as bodies formed around an elevated platform, allowing a performance to unfold. The Captain stayed with his ship and removed the gangplank in case of unwanted guests, while Annie, The General and Charles conversed among the various troupes in search of their friend, their loved one Stinky.

"Yes I know Stinky," said one young man. "As far as I'm aware he stayed in London, he was quite heavily involved in the rebellion, he's become quite a man." Soon more theatrical characters stumbled over to the visitors to give accounts on this mutual acquaintance.

"He leads a troupe that dwells within the sewers, who every night make their way to the surface of London's streets to perform, to give people a brief taste of freedom, a brief taste of expression."

"He's becoming folklore," whispered another.

The Seeds held complexions of sadness, each of them worried they would never see their friend again, this gentle, charismatic soul.

Applause gathered within their sombre surroundings as the performance came to an end and each actor gave their bow. The chance to display their talents once more was too much for Rimbaud's crew, they knew it was something they had to do.

" May we perform?" asked Annie to whom the crowd responded with pronounced enthusiasm, with immense anticipation, in wonder of what these strangers could achieve, what they could do. The Seeds would take all their pain and let it transcend into something beautiful, into a conceptualized form. A great purge awaited them. They decided upon Annie's very own three man play *The Mourning Day* a production deemed appropriate to the situation, a cathartic narrative based upon the idea of loss. Each performer delved into their characters as deep emotions began to arise for all to witness, for all to see. Their hearts palpitating against the flesh, beating against the surface.

The presence of night had slowly began to unveil itself when Rimbaud left the ship in search of his troupe, angered and frustrated with the hours that had been taken from him.

Then he saw it. Upon high terrain he saw a line of silhouettes, figures keeping watch, mounting horses, announcing their presence with a reflection of light, a reflection of sinister intention.

"We have to leave"

Rimbaud ran through the crowd, pushing past bonfires and human excrement before eventually finding his crew. The light was drawing closer as a large cavalry charged towards them, a surprise attack. The Dandy moved rapidly ahead, allowing his cane to sweep through the grey coloured realm of dusk, for he had not given up the chase, for he had not forgotten his prey.

"They're coming, everyone to their positions!"

The occupants had been awaiting this course of action, and were ready to fight, ready to win. Rimbaud and The seeds fled back towards their ship, back towards their escape, with a small crowd following them in pursuit. The charge had finally reached their enemy where a vicious battle ensued.

"We'll take as many as we can, but the ship can't hold many."

The Dandy was thrown from his horse and into the thick mud beneath him, as a squad of knife throwers formed a circle around his thin and now fragile frame.

"So you think you can all take me on? With pleasure."

The troupe made it back to the ship and one by one were allowed as many occupants onto the deck as possible. Smoke poured into the bloodied air as a huge fire began to take over the camp. For those who witnessed, for those who fought, it was a vision of hell.

"Charles raise the anchor, we can't possibly take anymore!"

The Dandy swiftly moved through each of his opponents, blocking and disarming each threat before allowing their bodies to fall into a bloodied pile of unconsciousness. He had their ship in sight, he had finally caught their scent, The General stared out back towards the camp, catching a glimpse of the man who had caused his friends so much misery, so much pain.

"I am disgraced, impeach'd and baffled here,
Pierced to the soul with slander's venom'd spear,
The which no balm can cure but his heart-blood
Which breathed this poison."

The General quickly made his way down to his quarters and retrieved the rifle which had been positioned beneath his bunk; he would end Thomas once and for all. The Dandy slowly battled his way across the uneven landscape, bringing himself closer and closer to the Odyssey, readying himself for the final confrontation.

"The croaking raven doth bellow for revenge"

With one deep breath The General took aim and fired his only shot, penetrating his target with ease. He had never lost his talent as a marksman, he now thought to himself, in awe of his own brutal deed. Thomas fell to his knees as a smirk drifted across his pale and cold complexion, forever lost to the fate that now awaited him.

"Such is life."

"The anchor's been raised Captain…lets go!" shouted Charles as the boat began to slowly pull itself away from the inferno that now besieged the land. Tears of pity and tears of woe filled the eyes of everyone onboard as they moved into the moonlight, as guilt leeched upon their thoughts. It was a day no one would forget. The Odyssey and her passengers were heading towards an unbeknownst future, towards a more passionate, more fulfilling life.

The Book Seller (A play)

Act one

The wind is heard, playing silently against the night. Jacque Burden walks against a canvas of black, slowly strolling through the East End docks to meet his accomplice and confidant Rimbaud. Before him blows the large sails of The Odyssey, while an aging gentleman smokes a cigarette, securing rope to a nearby bollard.

Jacque: Evening, I hope you had a pleasant journey

Rimbaud: Not at all my friend; I think we are going to have to draw a conclusion to this soon Jacque; the risks are becoming too great.

Jacque: What happened?

Rimbaud: I was raided by the river police; they didn't find any contraband but it was too close, I fear we may not be so lucky again.

Jacque: Maybe we should think about meeting in another part of the country, Whinstable perhaps?

Rimbaud: I don't know Jacque, I'm only doing this for the money, so one day I can settle down amongst nature and have a care free life, death or the confinement of a cell does not appeal to me.

Jacque: We just have to be more careful, this is important.

Rimbaud: It is important but I am not ready to become a martyr for it. I turned my back on poetry decades ago, I owe literature nothing.

Jacque: This is bigger than ourselves, we cannot let these parasites win, we need to keep these works alive.

Rimbaud: This is not your battle Jacque. Why don't you return to France and feel liberty once more, there is nothing keeping you here in this vacuous country, leave.

Jacque: I can't

Rimbaud: Then you must find someone else, this is my last run Jacque, I'm sorry, but it's getting too dangerous.

Jacque: No my friend, I understand your concerns, do you know anyone who may be willing to fulfil your role?

Rimbaud: I will write to you with the details of my friend Arthur, I'm sure he will be willing to take up your cause.

Jacque: That would be very much appreciated.

Rimbaud: I'm sorry Jacque; it has been a pleasure

Jacque: I'll be saddened not to be working with you anymore. Did you manage to get everything on the list?

Rimbaud: I did, my contact had some trouble locating *Beowulf*, but fortune found him in the end.

Jacque: I'm glad to hear it, how is James? Keeping well?

Rimbaud: He's recently become engaged to Mary, he seems to be very happy.

Jacque: I am very grateful to hear that news, shall we clarify that we have everything on the list?

Both men reach into their jacket pockets to pull out folded pieces of parchment.

Rimbaud: So I have

   - Four copies of *Dorian*
   - *Origin of Species*
   - *Beowulf*
   - *Madam Bovary*
   - *The Republic*
   - *Macbeth*
   - *Juliet*

   and a collection of Verlaine's

Jacque: That's everything.

Rimbaud: I have to go back to the ship to get them. When is the carriage arriving?

Jacque: It should be arriving in a few minutes; we should probably get moving.

Rimbaud: I will be back in a moment.

The wind kept playing its soft music as Rimbaud returned to the ship. Jacque looked down towards his pocket watch and began to move aimlessly, waiting for his friend and their carriage to arrive. The scenery has grown darker and the tension was building. Something does not sit right within the air of their surroundings.

Rimbaud: Here it is, me and my crew better take our leave, while we still can, this run doesn't feel right Jacque, There is something sinister in tonight's proceedings. Farewell old friend.

Jacque: How are your crew? Are they still missing being able to perform?

Rimbaud: I allow them to perform, to one another, in the streets of France. They can still fulfil their passion.

Jacque: I'm glad to hear it. Goodbye and I hope you have a safer return journey. All the best my friend.

The sound of the carriage beckoned them, thundering through the landscape before slowly coming to a halt at Jacque's side.

Rimbaud: Goodbye Jacque.

Jacque rapidly moves towards the carriage and swiftly pulls open the door. What he finds waiting for him pushes him back, slowly retreating towards Rimbaud's ship, his face stricken with fear.

Millar: Well well well, I finally have the pleasure of being greeted with your

presence Mr Burden; do you want to do this easily? (He says while exiting the carriage.)
The curtain falls.

Act three

Three men sit within a small meeting chamber at The Black museum. Millar, his superintendent Charles Anderson, and a senior politician, Lord Ashcroft. Each man graces their table with a complexion of complete devastation.
Lord Ashcroft: So you're telling me that somehow Jacque Burden, unassisted, was able to escape from The Dark Tower and leave absolutely no trace? Something suspicious is going on here.
Anderson: We are doing everything we can; no stone is being left unturned, every jailer is being interviewed as we speak.
Lord Ashcroft: Something needs to be done quickly; this Burden character has made a mockery of us all. He needs to be found and made an example of.
Anderson: We are doing everything we can my lord, you can be assured. Millar won't rest until we regain this villains capture.
Lord Ashcroft: I hope so, for both of your sakes. Did you get anything out of him when you had him under torture? You must have gathered some information surely?
Anderson: Mr Burden revealed information that led to the capture of an anarchist group known as the Rhymer's Club. They were planning on distributing verse; and we managed to stop their dangerous plot from unfolding, thanks to the tactics of Inspector Millar here.
Lord Ashcroft: What about this Rimbaud character? Did you get any information out of him? How about his crew, The Seeds?
Anderson: Most have been put through interrogation but too little effect. Theirs deaths will be taking place shortly.
Lord Ashcroft: And what of the others?
Anderson: We've had to send one, known as The General to Bedlam, he was too lost to the mind for interrogation. You can be assured he's suffering.
Lord Ashcroft: Millar, what is the next course of action?
Millar: He has connections to France, where he may be trying to flee. Every ship leaving our shores is being searched thoroughly, as is his cellar. Where

we have managed to retrieve many banned and corrosive artefacts.

Lord Ashcroft: The biggest bust in years I heard.

Millar: Indeed Sir

Anderson: I hope you get back to work with haste Millar. Maybe it's best you take your leave immediately.

Millar: Yes Sir

Millar slowly brought himself out of his chair and made his way back towards the door, before quietly shutting it behind him. The room was left in an immersion of intimidating silence.

Lord Ashcroft: If there are no results soon Anderson, he will be the one who suffers for it.

Anderson: I understand. (while nodding)

Lord Ashcroft: No one has escaped from The Dark Tower before. If he is not caught this could be something that develops within the imaginations of the populous. He could become a myth or legendary figure. We are in a dangerous situation Superintendent; I hope you understand the seriousness of this matter.

Anderson: I do my Lord; we are doing everything we can.

Suddenly gunshots breached their surroundings, penetrating the silence. Both Lord Ashcroft and Anderson stood immediately from their chairs, bound to stillness through the invasion of their fear.

Lord Ashcroft: What is going on!?

Minutes passed within the dwellings of their silence before a young officer forced himself into the room.

Officer: I'm sorry, it's Inspector Millar, he's been murdered.

The curtain falls

The Prisoner

The murderer was led back into the shadows of his cell, back into the shade of his feculent chamber, his sparse and sinister home. Iron shackles weighed heavy upon The Painter's thin and unnourished frame, dragging his chains across a sea of cold and damp stone, before seating himself back down upon the unwashed sheets of his bunk. Behind him stood a newly promoted inspector, watching his prisoner with a conspiratorial glare.

"Try to make yourself comfortable Mr Derchef," grinned Bartlett as he placed a cigarette between the lips of his smirk, "I hope you become satisfied within the walls of this abode."

After the murder, hundreds had filed past The Black Museum demanding to see the assassin, this face behind such a sinister deed, behind such a slaughter, with nothing coming to their avail. A haunting mystery was trying to be pieced together by the tongues of thousands, inside the minds of an inquisitive and slowly waking populous.

Franz had since dwelt within the confinements of an insufferable isolation, within a vacuum in which he felt the most intense and torturous agony. For most of his adult life he had felt alone, had felt unloved, choosing instead to lock himself away within the warmth of his studio, obsessed in his own self-absorbed creation, holding the reins to his own perceived world. Each stroke contained the fuel for catharsis, for salvation, each piece allowing The Painter to indulge within a brief sense of calm, within a brief sense of worth. Solitude is the chosen foundation to an artist, but now that it was forced upon him, it had become intolerable. Life for Franz was only to exist.

"Are you aware of why this place was named The Black Museum, Mr Derchef?" asked the inspector as he took small steps further into the cell, "I don't think many people do." Franz rubbed at his wrists where heavy iron ripped at his flesh, leaving dirty wounds to occupy his beaten and bruising body. The Prisoner's lips were dry as he gave a sullen and quiet response. "No…no I don't."

A small barred window sat high above, submerged within the thick texture of darkness, allowing faint traces of light to seep into the hopelessness of their occupant, of their sufferer. The Inspector dropped his cigarette and stamped out its flame as he began to give an answer.

"The Museum was named after the Great Purge of 1885...not only was the building a headquarters for the police, but also the main storage facility for the debauchery of the art form, the individualistic idea of expression, art Mr Derchef, rhyme, sculpture, all relics of our past. The subversive, the beautiful and the mundane, anything that could disrupt the rhythm of society, the structure of control."

Franz held onto the idea of the fate he felt awaited him, to be tried, sentenced and put to death, to be remembered by his muse, to be remembered through his art, to have given himself meaning. He wished to take his last lonesome breath with immediacy.

"A structure you have also wish to disrupt, isn't that right Mr Derchef?"
The Prisoner looked up towards a tall and stocky, middle aged man who for ten years had been working his way through roles within Her Majesty's Police, a careerist, a fiend. The Inspector stood in his well dressed, authoritive stance, awaiting his reply, while screams scratched into the sombre melodies of slamming doors and marching footsteps. The Prisoner looked down towards his bloodied dirt ridden feet.

"I didn't wish to disrupt anything...I just wanted his love."

"Yes, yes you've told us all about Lord Douglas's, but as a painter? You went against everything this reign stands for, discipline, honour, ideology; you've helped to undermine everything we have accomplished."

Franz closed his eyes as a gathering voice came closer towards his cell, as thick black liquid poured onto his hands and into the miserable narrative of his conclusion. He didn't have long to wait.

"I forgot to tell you, we've brought our special guest a present. I'm sure it's going to help you in your long stretch of confinement Mr Derchef, we hope you like it."

Upon the last word, three officers brought in a large framed portrait which was immediately hung within the shadows of The Painters seclusion.

"You will not be tried and no one will ever know of your existence, the reasons for your imprisonment, who carried out this violent and most despicable act."

Then he saw it, the face of his tormentor, the manifestation of an aching discomfort, his love, the body, the flesh of an aging Lord Douglas. Franz descended into a state of panic, immediately throwing himself into the air in a fit of outrage. "Kill me!"

The Inspector gave a sinister chuckle as he turned to leave, striking a match in preparation of lighting another cigarette. Never again will you leave this dungeon, this cell, any attempts to harm yourself or the painting will be met with severe punishment, do you understand?"

Franz threw himself to the floor as a beckoning burst of anguish infiltrated his confinement, catching the attention of two nearby officers and laughter to all those who were paying witness to this cruel and psychopathic act.

"A guard will be keeping watch at all times, goodbye Mr Derchef, as I said; I hope you soon grow to become fond of this place." The Inspector gave one last chuckle as he stepped back out into the passageway and the door was slammed shut and locked behind him. The last Franz would ever see of his victim's successor, his unsympathetic judge. Silence reigned once more as The Painter stared into the expression of his beloved, his infatuation, his eternal tormentor, Alfred.

Stinky's Troupe

Stinky stood in his pale complexion, with patchy white makeup and a fur plush top hat, the Ringmaster waited for his admirers, his loyal and impoverished audience. Warm air pushed past generous lips as a small stocky frame dressed in garments of hazel brown dungarees and matching corduroy jacket, rippled in the nightly wind, as wide spheres of darkest blue fell into a joyful stare of anxious anticipation, of intense elation.
"They're coming, they're coming, quickly everyone take your positions."

From deep beneath the cobbled surface rose the silhouettes of four wonderful people, four beautiful performers, moving with haste below the evening's last surviving lanterns, their newly borrowed stage. The congregation moved slowly through the shadows, through a lurid street moulded in bitterness, in hardship, ready for their confinements to be transformed into a spectacle, into a grand and fulfilling escape. A majestic medium dwelling within the untimely hour of midnight.

"I welcome you all to tonight's performance, we hope you enjoy the production and Shh… don't tell anyone." A gathering laughter moved through the sound of clapping hands as the troupe's ringmaster retired into the darkness, allowing Eva to take centre stage. She displayed her incredible physical flexibility, her extreme acrobatic talent; she was the group's contortionist, the group's most level headed thinker. Stinky was honoured to have been surrounded by such great showmen, by such good friends. There was Hercules the Giant, a man who took great pride in his strength, in his individualistic ability. With a looming and sinister nine foot structure, he struck fear into the hearts of many, holding an audience spellbound.
"Fee-fi-fo-fum
  I smell the blood of an Englishman
  Be he alive, or be he dead
  I'll grind his bones to make my bread."
There was Peter the Magician who perplexed a hundred gazing eyes with grand illusions, with a grand and hypnotic presence. A conjuror of impossible acts, of impossible outcomes.
"Ladies and Gentleman I will now evaporate from this very spot, I hope

you're watching closely..."

The narrow bindings of St Giles elevated with immense laughter as Stinky's favourite thespian took to the stage, a young boy named Charlie. He was a silent but charismatic performer, able to host a variety of emotions through the art of slapstick, through the art of mime, a brilliant and mesmerizing prodigy. The moonlight sharpened its stare as the performers grouped together to make their bow, to draw upon the breath of their catharsis, their applause, unknowingly captured within the sinister stare of a black Bombay cat.

The troupe looked upon one another for a collective agreement, on a course of action, should they deliver an encore?

"It's too dangerous, we've been here long enough, we have to be careful," exclaimed Peter, haunted by anxiety and suffocating within an air that had become thick with tension, "We should leave."

The chants grew louder as the troupe whispered among themselves, and a feline sprinted into the distance, ready to draw their nightly tale's conclusion.

"We shall give you one last performance," shouted the Ringmaster.

The crowd burst into applause, still not ready to be taken back into the confinements of their reality, their vacuous and bleakest prison.

"Charlie why don't you go again? You're the one they adore, the one they love."

Stinky had been inspired by his dearest soul mate, his closest friend, the late Leopold. A man who showed immense bravery, immense discipline, a man his troupe could not forget.

Since his vanishing, Leopold had become mythical, legendary, becoming the imagery of the mind, the imagery of dreams. Stinky wanted to follow in his footsteps, to create his own defining legacy, his own unvanquishable narrative.

"Run!"

The crowd hurriedly dispersed, chasing thin traces of light submerged within the shadows to find a way home, away from the gathering footsteps pacing towards their stage. The pack was being led by a strolling Bombay cat, an animal trained to seek out performers, to bring about their capture. Eva and Peter had hurriedly thrown themselves back into the sanctity of the sewers, back into their lurid abode, as truncheons surrounded Hercules and a vicious fight ensued.

Charlie led his master into an adjoining alleyway, pushing past the feculent pools of filth that littered the ground beneath them and while hounding constables grew closer in their pursuit, closer in their stare.

"Charlie go on without me, I can't keep up, get out of here!"

The young man swiftly turned around to see his friend pulled down into a thick layer of ashen white as three of Her Majesty's officers restrained their fugitive against the cold cobbled surface.

"Run Charlie...get out of here!" beckoned Stinky in agitation. "Carry on!"

Charlie took one last look at the man who had given him so much, his trade, his talents, his life.

The Astronomers nightmare

In Victorian Britain, unlike that on the continent, astronomy had become the domain of the wealthy amateur, of the wealthy outlaw. Commissioning telescopes and founding societies to unravel the secrets of the universe, to expand our factual mind and gather material to explain and theorize over. A dangerous occupation, a fulfilling and learned task.
"Henry take a look at this, isn't it incredible?"
Ms Elizabeth Whitaker had been reading Pierre- Simon Laplace's groundbreaking work *System of the World,* and through William Herschel's recommendation had been testing the theory their observed nebulae might be a new nascent solar system. The hypothesis dwelt within the idea that the apparent swirling patterns captured in the heavens were composed of gas and dust condensing into a star, and debris from the outer edges would eventually become planets, a fascinating spectacle, a fascinating idea.
"Oh my Ms Whitaker, I haven't seen anything like it."

Their observatory allowed them to stare into the vast depths of darkest space in search of contemporary wonder, of greater understanding. Their brass and japanned steel telescope, held upon a steel pivot and hardwood tripod had become a gateway to new worlds, to new destinations. Its lens gathering light for their viewers, gifting them with a brighter, clearer, more magnified image. Astronomy allowed Elizabeth's soul to transcend her place, to look upwards and find another, to look out upon things beyond her grasp, out towards the aesthetic of life itself. She was compelled in the pursuit of discovery, in the pursuit of knowledge, and in her lifetime had built up a vast and extensive library. Containing everything from ancient playwrights, to philosophy, to latest ideas born out of science, out of study. Elizabeth wanted to know the unknown, whatever that maybe.
"Will you please file the notes I have taken Henry, I'd like to go over them in the morning."
"As you wish Ms Whitaker."

The observatory dwelt within a luxurious central London penthouse, and was decorated by gold tinted candlelight, which burned solemnly into the early hours. Elizabeth couldn't help but take one last look through her telescope, her most cherished possession, to take one last look towards the grandest and most intriguing of mysteries. Then she saw it, the event that would change her life forever.

"Oh my."

Through the winter streets of Notting Hill, a carriage had been summoned, to take Ms Whitaker straight to the president of the astronomical society, a Professor Joseph May. She hadn't been able to sleep, her thoughts woven into the imagery of what she had seen, what she had witnessed, out there within the ever expanding horizon of space. Elizabeth was taken to the impoverished dwellings of Kentish town, to meet this once great intellectual, this aging lifelong academic. Joseph poured himself a small glass of whisky and sat himself down in an armchair opposite. His thin frame and pale complexion painted a portrait in Ms Whitakers mind; it was one of sadness and despair, a withering heart bruising within the cruelty of his existence.

"How can I be of service to you? Aren't we meeting in a few days?"

Elizabeth tapped her fingertips in immense anticipation, she wanted to tell him everything that she'd seen, to dissect the finest details and bring her past to life, but she knew she couldn't. For although the professor was a friend, he was a competitor, a rival.

"I need to know how to publish a new discovery, a new finding? I have absolutely no idea when it comes to the administrative side of things. Any information you can give me would be extremely appreciated." The professor looked towards his guest with sullen intrigue, with a bewildering resentment. "Can you tell me what it is you claim to have found?" He asked while slowly taking a sip from the glass he had rested upon an undernourished leg. "I'm enticed."

"I can't Professor."

Joseph sat silent, looking out towards his miserable and bleakest surroundings, through the window of a dirty, filth ridden home.

"Are you aware of the repercussions such knowledge holds Ms Whitaker? This could change everything."

For weeks the astronomer and her butler gazed upon the nocturnal tides of their nightly sky, documenting their observations in the finest detail, in the most intricate fashion. It wouldn't be long before they could unleash it upon her peers, upon humanity.

"This is what I will be remembered for Henry, this is groundbreaking."
Elizabeth had left The Painted Theatre in the early hours of a Tuesday
morning with surrounding friends, her loved ones, having become gripped by
a contemporary production of Shakespeare's *Taming of the Shrew*, growing
popular amongst the theatre growing public.
"That was exquisite; we may have to see it again!"
A shared carriage had dropped them a short walk away from each of their
residences, sharing farewells as they stumbled into their separate directions,
into separate lives.
"Goodbye to you all, I shall see you soon!"
Ms Whitaker had been graced with accomplishment, with a profound joy, a
smile crossing her face as she wandered home in her inebriated state, her
celebratory manner. For the first time having something to live for, a reason to
exist. Elizabeth moved through the narrow immersions of darkness when she
saw a strange figure, staring towards her belligerent stride, her intoxicated
complexion. Wearing a long black velvet cloak, the sinister creature stood
silent and still, only turning their head when the astronomer moved quietly
past them, it was the imagery of a nightmare, the imagery of a dream.
Elizabeth immediately removed her key and hurriedly unlocked the door to
her abode, slamming it shut behind her and running up the cold, creaking
steps. Heavy breaths panted through her lungs as she made her way into the
living quarters, and into the safety of her home.
"Henry…Henry!"
The shades that dwelt within her confinement brought a fearful anxiety, a
fearful gaze, as silence crept through the hallway of Elizabeth's night, a
petrifying and foreboding presence.
"Henry…"

She could distinctly hear a howling wind, giving the windows sound in its
ferocious force, in its sweeping aggression. Ms Whitaker ran through their
opaque hallway towards her loyal butler, towards her most abiding servant,
pushing her way into his room to find a deeply sinister sight, the most
grotesque act of destruction.
Before her on the bed laid a body, visible within the room's candlelight, the
bloodied and punctured flesh of her friend, her assistant. Ms Whitaker
submerged in tears ran into the living quarters to check on the strange figure

that had dwelt outside. She pushed her fingers between the curtains and stared out into the nocturnal landscape, but he was nowhere to be seen, slowly turning round to then be met with a crippling sight, her stranger.

"Is it me you seek?"

A plague had come to strengthen Elizabeth's vision, able to gaze upon her menace in his full form within the darkness, within the lurid veil of her chamber; fear had kept Ms Whitaker still.

"Do you know why I am here?"

The astronomer moved towards the spiral staircase, towards her observatory, as the stranger pulled out a long sharp object from the confinement of his belt and held it tight within his grasp.

"Do you?"

Elizabeth let out a loud scream before gathering her courage, providing a defiant stance to converse with her murderer, this fiend.

"Why did you kill Henry? Why?"

The stranger graced his victim with a scarred smirk, resting his eyes upon a heretic, a blasphemous skin, wanting Ms Whitaker to be ridden of her life, her heresy. He rested the knife at his side.

"We intercepted letters from your friend, your mentor, a Professor Joseph May." Elizabeth listened with intrigue and with morbid inquisitiveness.

"All over the country he has written to many academic acquaintances, informing them of a discovery, one founded by you Ms Whitaker, a discovery you plan to publish. We needed to know what that was."

Without thought Elizabeth looked up towards the observatory.

"Your papers have already been burnt to ash, no one will ever know your name... your findings. You're destined for the knife Ms Whitaker...my knife."

The astronomer trembled with despair.

"Why?"

The stranger gave his final smirk, slowly lifting the knife to unveil itself before him. No one would ever know the name Ms Elizabeth Whitaker, nor what she had discovered.

The artist reveals beautiful things, revealing all to the world, to the audience she loves.

Life had become her subject matter, her muse for creation, and a show that was about to begin.

Oil lamps glowed softly against the scarlet mould of their grand surroundings, as hundreds gathered to take their seats within a swarm of anticipation, of unbeknownst intrusiveness, ready for the spectacle that awaited them. The Verite Theatre had been situated within the Pigalle district of Paris and had become an abode to the exiled, to the sanctity of creation, fulfilling the hearts and minds of an audience, of its artists.

Fragmentations of subconscious had furiously inked their way onto a blank page, cultivating in a collection of non- linear narrative, of shattered thought, ready to be bound to the concentration of the populous, to the confinement of history, becoming their character's incarnation, their theatrical revenant.

"This is a wonderful and magnificent dedication to those we have lost Isabel, I'm proud of you."

The curtains opened to a backdrop of silhouettes, shaped into the structure of London's most celebrated monuments, the Dark Tower and Nelson's Column posed in their infamous iconography, as Alberto recited the productions opening monologue and the whispering crowds grew silent.

"We hope you enjoy the production and shh…don't tell anyone."

Assembling laughter had been gathered in Stinky's words once more as their actor left the stage and back into the shade of a collaborator's nerves, of a director's fear. The scenery of a twisted landscape reined in the horror of another world, of another place, as their viewers stared in trepidation towards an upcoming act.

The couple had been intricate during their casting process, having each performer naturally hold the charisma and mannerisms of each individual personified. They wanted perfection, to be transported back into the imagery of their past, their nightmares. To them writing was to purge, a catharsis, to bring their dreams into the tangible reign of reality.

William and Isabel had immersed themselves in all that their new city had to offer. Finding themselves caught between the notes of beautiful melodies, within the deeper thought of word, but never forgetting The seeds, nor their life before the convenience of a dawn.

Isabel's friends had always invaded the hour of her sleep, the hour of her fragility; she could never truly escape the flesh of her past, and the spirits haunting her present. The script had become her refuge, her salvation.

"Until now, since the day I first met you…
I have only loved Isabel."

Then something miraculous happened. As the playwrights peered out into the audience they saw a man each of them thought to be someone they recognised, someone well acquainted with, The General.

"No it can't be, it's not possible."

They stared through hundreds of complexions, guiding their eyes over a host of admirers, soon to be catching sight of Annie, Charles and a smartly dressed Lord Douglas.

"William they've made it, they've made it here!"

Each member of the troupe had smiles lifting from their faces as they saw themselves as characters, having been glorified in such a flattering and beautiful way. "They made it here in time to see your work finally come alive Isabel; they'll know you've been thinking of them." Joy rushed through their bodies in the elation of what they had seen; it wouldn't be long before they would all be together again.

"It is not in the stars to hold our destiny, but ourselves." Bellowed George in his character as an aging and insane Shakespearian actor,

"And this our life, exempt from public haunt
  Finds tongues in trees, books in the running brookes
  Sermons in stones, and good in everything."

Isabel watched as she played puppet master to her friend's deepest emotions before the cast came back on stage to make their bow, receiving the most deserving applause. They were given a standing ovation and a host of cheers which grew further as Isabel walked out onto the stage.

She looked at each of her friends with gratitude, with pride, before she saw him, hiding in the shadows, the man she thought she'd lost, the notorious Jacque Burden. She felt the most intense happiness, the most intense elation, excitable for the future and all it might bring.

My humble friends are here once more
Gentle, honest and kind
Having been adrift over a darkened sea
And the moonlights glittered shine

Their roots were held in misery
Bringing joy to you and me
These courageous dancing stars
O the flowers they've grown to be

Allow these eyes to perceive the heart
To allow a triumphant gaze
To gift the world with expression
Where the streets became their stage

We'll never forget the name Leopold
The performer of a bygone day
Nor his friend Stinky
Who perfected each of his display's

An abode held in darkness
That had drenched the vacuous hour
Had found and sought its salvation
In a city laden with flowers.

A Conclusion With Charlie Chaplin

Charlie stared intently at each frame of celluloid, carefully combining each shot into a linear sequence, pursuing the creation of a motion picture, a lasting and thought- provoking narrative. Editing had often been described as being unique to cinema, separating itself from anything that had preceded it, "the invisible art." The job of an editor was not just to cut off film slates or edit dialogue scenes but to creatively work with layers of images and pacing, drawing parallels with that of the novelist, or the poet, effectively remoulding the work into a cohesive whole, something their audience could be drawn into, become engaged with. With the invention of the splicer and threading machine, the process sped up rapidly, making the cut cleaner, more precise. Despite his successful life in America and the riches he possessed, the artist never forgot where he came from, what forged him into a rebel, a defiant performer; he wanted to change the world, to change humanity.

"If this is the end, then we'll give him something meaningful to say, something true."

Charles Spencer Chaplin had been born on the 16th April 1889 to an actress, an outlaw, Hannah Hill, who for years lived within the grip of poverty and hardship. As a child, he had been taken to The Painted Theatre to witness his mother perform, to grace the stage alongside legends such as Leopold and the charismatic clown Stinky.

"I have a good feeling about you young man; I'll be watching you closely."

At this early age, Charles had already begun his apprenticeship, having watched each manoeuvre, each act with the strictest intensity, allowing his eyes to pick up each charismatic trait, his legs impersonating each and every dance. These were the faces of his heroes, his dreams. Hannah having grown ill with madness had been sectioned at the notorious Bedlam Hospital, the building of nightmares, an inhumane prison to the sufferers, to agony. To avoid the workhouse, Charles had been taken into the furthest depths of the sewers as part of Stinky's troupe, as part of his family, within the stench of a lurid underground city.

"You were magnificent tonight my boy…extraordinary."

Each of his new friends were inspired by the tales of Leopold, of his legendary shows. A man who brought joy to the poor, to the squalor of despair, a man all of them wished to emulate.

"What was it like performing with him?"

The Ringmaster often recounted his life with The Seeds to his loyal thespian's, unfolding the love of William and Isabel and the Shakespearian recitals of The General. His listener's were in awe and their imagery helped to feed their imagination. Together they performed over a hundred shows, bringing a spectacle to thousands, but it wasn't to last, it wasn't to be. Charlie was the only one that got away. For weeks he drifted through London's streets, through the starvation of destitution, through a desperate mind. He had been briefly taken under the wing and mentored by a prize fighter called Bull, the inspiration behind Charles Reisner's character as the Bully in the 1921 film *The Kid*. He was picked up by a troupe of travelling mimes known as "Zazou." who together finely dressed in fur plush top hats, pale makeup and tails toured the country in their carriages, bringing a show to those who needed it most, those in the most desperate of spirits. They performed at the various camps that had been scattered across the country, Portsmouth and Dover, the docks of Scotland, having always received the friendliest welcomes, their most honoured audiences. The troupe had never spoken to one another, instead only communicating through expression, through movement. Within months, Charlie had become a master of his craft, having the ability to influence within a silent world, to entertain.

"Are you sure about this Charlie?" When this is released they are going to come after you with everything they've got. Are you sure you want that?" Flickers of light projected smooth images onto the far wall of the editing suite, as the artist looked upon his most beloved character, his icon, the Tramp. After years in residence at a theatre in the heart of London's underworld, Charlie had been invited to tour America, where he would see his first ever film and subsequently come to star in this new art form, this pioneering medium. With the help of his first director Mack Sennet Charlie was able to fully form the character that would stay with him throughout his career. He took inspiration from the impoverishment of Leopold, of Stinky, and the underground network of artists that had buried themselves within the remains of a far away city. He wanted to symbolize his friends, their cause and celebrate their courage. He too would also be willing to take up the fight. "We can't release this…what are you doing!"

The Immigrant caused outrage, an attack upon the establishment and their cruelty; it was a precursor to many films that would take this stance, this critical attitude. *Modern Times* explored the fundamental principles of capitalism, of man becoming machine, the oppressive nature of big business. The rich were his villains of choice, the nemesis to a loveable and forever charming hero.

"He's attacking the United States, he's dangerous to the patriotic idealism of this country, I want everything we have on him." The artist's rebellious stance had brought him to the attention of the FBI, of a one J. Edger Hoover.

"I don't like this clown one bit, he's a dirty, filthy red." There was so much more to Charlie's films, so much beauty, so much poetry, inspired by the playwright William Caswell and his saddening romantic verse, his use of elevated realism. The Tramp would never get the girl, and like William had used his art form to write an ode to the woman he loved, to his everlasting muse. He was an optimist, a representative of the underprivileged.

"The whole point of the little fellow is that no matter how down on his ass he is, no matter how well the jackals succeed in tearing him apart, he's still a man of dignity."

The time had come to perform his most dangerous act, to give a speech that he hoped would shake the foundations of establishments throughout the world, succumbing to the humanity he had always sought, had always strived towards. Although the film was banned throughout Britain, underground screenings had been established in cities across the country, showing the latest works coming out of Europe, out of America. Charlie Chaplin had a message, one that would come to life in his film, *The Great Dictator.*

"I'm sorry, but I don't want to be an emperor. That's not my business. I don't want to rule or conquer anyone. I should like to help everyone - if possible - Jew, Gentile - black man - white." Audiences gathered in wonder, the first time they had ever heard his voice, through the gentle flow of his meaningful and hope filled words.

"Even now my voice is reaching millions throughout the world - millions of despairing men, women, and little children - victims of a system that makes men torture and imprison innocent people." The audiences across London looked upon one another, uncomfortable in small, smoke- ridden backrooms, in fear of being discovered, in fear of their confinement.

"To those who can hear me, I say - do not despair. The misery that is now upon us is but the passing of greed - the bitterness of men who fear the way of human progress. The hate of men will pass, and dictators die, and the power they took from the people will return to the people." Government officials from Britain had been sent a copy of the film and along with the FBI became sickened, succumbed with dread.

"Then - in the name of democracy - let us use that power - let us all unite. Let us fight for a new world - a decent world that will give men a chance to work - that will give youth a future and old age a security. By the promise of these things, brutes have risen to power. But they lie! They do not fulfil that promise. They never will!"

Countries feared the power he held, the influence he possessed. He was giving a speech that was helping to unify the underclass, the oppressed. They needed to neutralize this dissident threat.

"Let us fight to free the world - to do away with national barriers - to do away with greed, with hate and intolerance. Let us fight for a world of reason, a world where science and progress will lead to all men's happiness. Soldiers! In the name of democracy, let us all unite!"

Crowds had gathered together in a global experience, together stamping their feet in a powerful applause, they knew something had to be done.

17241348R00045

Printed in Great Britain
by Amazon